RAINEY

WITH A

CHANCE

OF

HALE

R. E. BRADSHAW

Titles from R. E. Bradshaw Books

Rainey Bell Thriller Series:
Relatively Rainey (2015) Lambda Literary Awards Finalist
Carl of the Bells (2015) (Short Story-eBook only)
Colde & Rainey (2014)
The Rainey Season (2013) Lambda Literary Awards Finalist
Rainey's Christmas Miracle (2011) (Short Story-eBook only)
Rainey Nights (2011) Lambda Literary Awards Finalist
Rainey Days (2010)

The Adventures of Decky and Charlie Series:
Out on the Panhandle (2012)
Out on the Sound (2010)

Molly: House on Fire (2012)
Lambda Literary Awards Finalist

Before It Stains (2011)

Waking Up Gray (2011)

Sweet Carolina Girls (2010)

The Girl Back Home (2010)

RAINEY
with a
CHANCE
of
HALE

A Rainey Bell Thriller

R. E. BRADSHAW

Published by
R. E. BRADSHAW BOOKS

USA

RAINEY with a CHANCE of HALE
By R. E. Bradshaw

© **2017 by R. E. Bradshaw. All Rights Reserved.**
R. E. Bradshaw Books/March 2017
ISBN-13: 978-0-9989549-2-9

Website: http://www.rebradshawbooks.com
Facebook: https://www.facebook.com/rebradshawbooks
Twitter @rebradshawbooks
Blog: http://rebradshawbooks.blogspot.com
For information contact rebradshawbooks@gmail.com

Acknowledgments

I would like to acknowledge the universe and the people in it that make me smile when I don't want to, laugh when I feel like crying, and see me through the good and the bad. I want to acknowledge that I am human, I make mistakes, and I strive to do better every day. I acknowledge that sitting at a computer writing about life all day is great, but living a life to write about is better. I acknowledge that I took some time to find stable legs again, to appreciate a soft place to land again, and to value the wisdom that comes with loss.

About the book...

Rainey Bell, a former FBI Behavioral Analyst, has had a couple of quiet years since her last brush with death. Her old teammate with the BAU and her children's Godfather, Danny McNally, pays a visit to North Carolina from Quantico to escort Rainey into the Butner Federal Correctional Complex.

Rainey made a promise almost twenty years ago to a distraught mother of a missing child. The opportunity to fulfill that pledge, one she should never have made, presents itself in the form of Chance Obadiah Hale. The teenager Rainey believed responsible for Alyson Grayson's disappearance was now a man in prison who wanted to talk, but only to Rainey.

Can Rainey and Danny finally get to the truth about Alyson and Chance? Or will Rainey's stubborn belief in his guilt put everyone she loves in mortal danger? Eeny, meeny, miny, moe. Who will be the first to go?

REB

Dedicated to dear friends.
You know who you are.
No hour too late.
No distance too far.

PART I

"Ah! well a-day! what evil looks
Had I from old and young!
Instead of the cross, the Albatross
About my neck was hung."
— Samuel Taylor Coleridge,
The Rime of the Ancient Mariner

1

January 1, 1998
Hale Trucking Maintenance Garage
CANAMEX Corridor Division
Pembina, North Dakota

Alyson Grayson flinched when the shotgun blast erupted behind her.

"You're an hour late," she said to the young man holding the smoking weapon. "Midnight has come and gone. It's the New Year already."

The handsome teen broke the old shotgun barrel open, then popped out the spent shell and tossed it over his shoulder. He took a deep drag off the joint he had been holding to his lips and blew pot smoke rings into the air, much to Alyson's delight. He smiled at her, blew the hot ashes from the joint, and then inserted the glowing red tip into his mouth. With the unlit end of the joint protruding from his lips, he placed his mouth close to hers. Puffing his cheeks, he blew slowly, which forced a thick stream of white smoke toward Alyson's waiting lips. She giggled, then opened her mouth and inhaled.

Alyson exhaled slowly, as she turned in circles and watched the Northern Lights dance in the sky above her. Her mother said she came into the world with a look of wonder on her face as if she was surprised to be there.

Her father would laugh and say, "Alyson approaches life in a constant state of 'wow.'"

She was almost fifteen and not above a bent rule or two. She made pretty decent grades and stayed out of trouble. Her mom and dad trusted her to make appropriate decisions, which she did for the most part. On occasion, she smoked a little pot, but not much, and she never drank alcohol.

Her parents would not arrive home from attending the Grayson family's annual New Year's Eve party until after the traditional sunrise sober-up breakfast. Alyson had asked to stay home so that she could attend the ice skating party on the small lake in the woods behind their house. The New Year's Eve bonfire was a local high school tradition she had finally aged into. Her promise to be home by 1:30 a.m. was in jeopardy the moment she decided to offer Chance Hale a ride home on her four-wheeler.

Chance was trouble. He was also her closest neighbor. Alyson's home was about a half-mile down the road from his. In her rural community, all the kids used four wheelers for travel through the trails and fields before acquiring driver's licenses. When Alyson saw Chance walking toward his home from the party, she slipped away from her friends to ask if he wanted a ride. She had been thrilled when he accepted.

"Come on," the still pot-smoking teen said, as he held open the door to the huge maintenance garage of Hale Trucking. "Let's go inside."

The door slammed shut behind them. The sound clapped like thunder through the cavernous building. Somewhere deep in Alyson's brain, the lizard awoke. Innate fears—fight or flight instincts—startled a recoiling reflex from her body.

The teen following her chuckled.

"A little jumpy, aren't you?"

"Yeah, I guess so," Alyson replied a tad awkwardly. "I should probably get home."

He stuck the joint in between her lips and smiled down at her, "The party's just started, darlin'."

Alyson told herself to chill out, took another drag, and followed Chance to a restored 1951 Chevy truck. The pot began masking the lizard brain alarms and loosened her tongue. She puffed and passed off the joint while walking around what she knew to be Chance's most prized possession.

"Wow, dude. You finished it. This is so sweet."

She smiled over at Chance, whose facial expression was lost in the shadow of the hoodie he wore under his bulky jacket. He nodded affirmation.

"Will you take me for a ride? Not right now, but soon."

She heard him answer flatly, "Yeah, I guess."

Chance was different from the other boys Alyson had toyed with since she discovered she could. He was mysterious and brooding, with an air of aloofness she found intriguing. Chance didn't look like the familiar North Dakota boys, with his lean, surfer-boy body and long blond ponytail. He pulled off the pouty, ruggedly handsome, untamed rebel look with the casualness that made it authentic. Alyson had recently discovered Chance Hale defined her "type."

Chance was a loner, a nonconformist—the kind of bad boy that made temptation stronger than the fear of her parents' reprisal. They were not as impressed with the young man who made no excuses for his drinking, smoking, and lack of conformity to society's rules, particularly the ones about school attendance. Alyson was already smitten enough to overlook these glaring flaws. To her, Chance seemed sad and lonely. With the blindness of the beauty for the beast, she thought she could heal his wounds.

He opened the tailgate of the pickup truck. The pot, mixed with the alcohol he reeked of, seemed to make Chance less communicative by the moment. Alyson began to think he had forgotten she was there. He sat down on the tailgate and then reclined back into his heavy parka in the bed of the truck. The warm garage seemed to lull him to sleep almost instantly.

"Well, I guess he won't freeze in here," she said. "I suppose I should get home now."

Before she could move, Alyson heard what sounded like a woman's muffled scream. Her head turned with the sound. She focused on the rear of a box truck parked about twenty-five feet away.

"Did you hear that?"

Chance was already snoring.

Perhaps it was because she was high or maybe it was the fact Alyson was just young and innocent enough to dismiss potential danger—for whatever reason, she crossed the floor to the box truck without the slightest concern for her safety.

"I swear I heard someone in there," she commented, as she surveyed the chained and locked rear doors of the truck.

The muffled cry came again. This time Alyson was sure it came from inside the truck.

As she turned, she said, "You heard that, didn't yo—"

Alyson's words were forcefully cut off in mid-syllable. She had no time to gasp, as the forearm closed around her neck and a hand clamped over her mouth. The strength of the man overpowered the petite teenager with ease.

She felt the words whispered against her cheek, "Yes, I heard it, but I wish you hadn't."

The forearm clamped down harder. It stopped the blood flowing to the previously alarmed lizard. The options of fight or flight were no longer available. The lizard switched focus to preservation mode and went silent. Wearing much the same look of surprise she wore at birth, Alyson Grayson saw a tunnel of darkness showered with falling stars.

She thought, "Wow."
And then she thought nothing.

2

"It's cold enough to freeze off body parts."

Chance Hale ignored the federal agent seated on the other side of the kitchen table. The sixteen-year-old pressed on his temples with the palms of his hands, in what appeared to be an attempt to keep the contents of his skull inside.

FBI Special Agent Rainey Bell noted the pot resin stains on his index finger and thumb, the reek of stale cigarettes, and the nauseating stench of booze-laced puke-breath. While they waited for his father to come back from the garage with the other agent, Rainey kept the hung-over teenager talking. Rather, she talked, and he tried to remain upright.

Chance Hale was in deep trouble. A suspect in the disappearance of his fourteen-year-old neighbor, Alyson Grayson, he was connected by proximity to the two frozen bodies recently discovered in the lake behind his home. Two frozen bodies and a missing girl resulted in FBI involvement. Chance didn't seem the least bit concerned.

Rainey looked out the window over the sink, continuing her weather observations, "Still spitting snow at zero degrees." She glanced back at Chance. "What did they say the wind chill was—minus twenty-one? I could be out there, what, thirty minutes before my face froze? This is just nuts. Pulling me from Louisiana to the frozen tundra—I don't think a prank deserved this assignment."

Rainey saw a brief millisecond of eye contact. Chance took notice that she may be a fellow rule breaker.

"I've only been here a week. The bureau said I was transferred to fill a temporary vacancy. I'm calling bullshit on that one. It was that picture of super-agent Walsh standing in his front yard in his boxers that landed me here."

Rainey made quote marks in the air and mocked the man she imitated with, "Mr. 'My Security System Can't Be Compromised.' Ha!"

She flashed a self-satisfied smile at Chance. "Patriarchal narcissism is why I am here. Guys like him can't abide being wrong or laughed at. I proved the one and certainly did the other."

She waited for a comment, a nod, anything, but received only a vacant teenage stare. Forced to resume her monologue, she continued the tale of her removal to the frozen tundra.

"I suppose his being my supervisor brought with it a tad of insubordination. But, you know, sometimes you have to show a braggart he isn't all that smart to make a point. Of course, the FBI frowns on that particular type of behavioral modification technique. Thus, here I sit with you freezing my ass off."

Nothing, no reaction, not even a hint of a smile. Chance closed his eyes and rubbed his temples with his fingertips.

Rainey tried another tack. "You moved up here from North Carolina, didn't you? Hillsborough, right? I grew up in Chapel Hill."

A grunt was Chance's only response, but he did respond. Progress had been made. Rainey abandoned her attempt to bond over shared nonconformist attitudes and stuck with their childhoods in warmer climes.

"You understand it takes time to adjust from coastal temps to 'Oh, my God! I'm freezing my tits off,' don't you?"

"I don't have tits," the slump-shouldered teen said, still rubbing his temples.

"Balls then," Rainey replied, dropping the "we can be friends" tone from her voice and adding, "Most mammals have tits, male and female. Unless you're a platypus or a species of rodent, you have them too. I'm assuming you didn't pay much attention in biology class—if you ever went."

Chance stretched and yawned over a barely concealed, "Fuck you."

It crossed Rainey's mind that young Chance Hale needed to be reminded of the seriousness of his situation. He was the last person seen with Alyson Grayson and professed to have no memory of the early morning hours of New Year's Day when she disappeared. The FBI was now at his home at the crack of dawn. If none of that raised young Chance's heart rate, Rainey had to wonder what would? She pondered the idea that he was either a cold-blooded killer devoid of empathy, or he was just a drunk, drugged-out teenager with detachment issues.

It was well known that Chance drank excessively. Three days ago, he dropped out of school on his sixteenth birthday, though he had attended only enough to avoid a truancy charge. He worked as a mechanic on his family's fleet of long-haul trucks. According to a completely frustrated and candid school counselor, the old pickup truck he restored seemed to be all that Chance cared about.

"He's too smart to drop out like this," the counselor said. "If he'd just sober up and try a little harder, he could do anything he wanted. He was in our school system for only three semesters. He was already in academic trouble when he enrolled."

The counselor pulled a folder from one of the file cabinets lining the wall in her office.

"Let me just check my file."

She read, silently nodding in agreement with her notes before she looked up and finished her assessment of young Mr. Hale.

"What I can tell you by law is that I believe his mother leaving when he was four years old did severe damage to such a young boy. I recommended to his mostly absent father that he get Chance into rehab and counseling. He refused to take the list of therapists I offered. It's just a shame, really. Chance can be quite charming and engaging when he wants to be. Just ask that gaggle of girls that swoon every time he walks by."

After an initial witness interview with Chance, who was not an official suspect at the time, he refused further questioning from Rainey and Supervisory Special Agent Stanley Hébert. Chance claimed his long-haul truck-driving father advised against it. Hébert, who had been observing Chance, was convinced it was not a coincidence two other bodies had been found behind his home.

"I know it in my bones, Bell. Something's wrong in that house," he said the previous evening when he dropped her back at the office. With his graying temples reflecting the car's dome light, he declared, "I'm not going to let that son of a bitch get away with killing those girls."

She'd only known SSA Hébert for seven days, but she liked him. She liked him enough not to be snarky when he called her hotel room in Grand Forks before dawn.

"Bell, get downstairs. We have to run up to Pembina. Locals say Joshua Hale came home about two this morning."

"What time is it now?" Rainey had to ask because her eyes were not yet cooperating. They only burned and watered from lack of sleep on the unfamiliar hotel mattress, when she tried to focus on the bedside clock.

"It's five a.m. The snow will slow us down a bit, but if we're on the road in thirty, we can be there by sunrise."

"I'll be down in fifteen," Rainey said, coming fully awake.

7

"Dress accordingly, we're in for negative temps today."

Rainey chuckled. "This adds a whole new level to being frozen out."

Hébert, in standard North Dakota form, answered, "It's not so bad. You'll get used to it."

"I don't want to be here long enough to get used to it," Rainey said without thinking.

"Well now, Special Agent Bell, you should have thought of that while you were down in the sunny south and before you told your last supervisor to 'lighten up.' Care to piss off two in a row?"

Rainey wasn't about to let her career crash over a prank. She responded with a crisp, "No, sir. I'll be right down."

After a harrowing drive up US Highway-29, even with an experienced North Dakota winter driver, they arrived just as the sun began to rise. The ruse for a visit was a verification of the whereabouts of all males in the vicinity the night of Alyson Grayson's disappearance, but they really wanted another crack at Chance. In his previous interviews, he had informed them that his dad was in Canada on a short run and didn't make it back until the afternoon on the first day of 1998. Joshua Hale left again before Alyson was reported missing and had been on the road until late last night.

The polite knock garnered no interest from the occupants of the Hale home. The much more intrusive cop knock brought a woman wearing a turban and face cream to the door, where two freezing but smiling federal agents greeted her. She was tall and a redhead, judging by the curl peeking from the headdress. That's about all Rainey could say about her, other than she looked unhappy to be answering the door at the crack of dawn.

"It's a little early. What can I do for you?" she asked, tugging the thick robe tighter against the cold seeping under the storm door.

"Good morning. I'm SSA Hébert. Are you Jean Berry? I believe we've spoken on the phone."

"Yes, Agent Hébert. How can I help you?"

"I'm here to see Joshua."

"Wait here. I'll get him," she replied, in an accent Rainey recognized as originating in the Piedmont area of North Carolina.

"Who was that?" Rainey asked.

Hébert's answer formed a trail of smoke, as he said, "Jean Berry. She works for Hale Trucking. That garage out back keeps their rigs on the road. Ms. Berry is here from the Carolina office to do parts inventory and accounting work for the shop. She does that about once a month. She has a private apartment and an office in the basement."

Rainey wondered why she hadn't seen anything about Jean Berry in Hébert's case notes, or why this was the first she knew of a private apartment. He seemed to read her expression.

"This house was searched top to bottom. Alyson is not here."

"What did she tell you about New Year's Eve?"

"She wasn't here that night. I verified with the home office in North Carolina that she drove up the next day after Alyson was reported missing. She answered the phone a time or two when I called to ask about Mr. Hale's whereabouts. She's usually a little nicer, but I guess it is early."

Rainey didn't think Jean Berry was all that "nice," having left them to freeze on the steps until Joshua Lee Hale came to the door.

"Good morning, Mr. Hale. Sorry to knock so early, but you're a hard man to catch at home. I'm Supervisory Special Agent Hébert with the FBI, and this is Special Agent Bell. Do you mind if we come in out of the cold to chat for a few minutes? It won't take long."

Hébert managed an invitation to the kitchen and scored a couple of hot cups of coffee, while he cagily pried information from Joshua Hale. Rainey admired Hébert's non-confrontational style and relaxed into the role of quiet sidekick. She mostly watched Chance, who reluctantly joined them at his father's request. The redhead had not reappeared.

"I got my logbook out in the cab of my truck. It'll show when I entered the country from Canada on New Year's Day," Joshua said, as a way to back up his alibi. "I was on a run to Mexico City and stopped by the house for a couple of hours, then I was back on the road."

Joshua started for the back door when Hébert asked, "May I come with you? I'd like to see this truck Chance restored. I hear it's something." He turned back to Chance. "A '51 Chevy 3100, five-window, right?"

Chance only grunted, which Rainey was learning was his preferred response.

"He ain't much for conversation in the mornings," Joshua said of his son, almost apologetically.

While Hébert and Joshua Hale left to recover the trucker's logbook from the eighteen-wheeler parked in the massive garage behind the house, Rainey was left with the insolent teenage boy. After nearly five years as a federal agent questioning cunning criminals, she knew how to handle the disrespectful, rebellious type. She figured Hébert had left her alone with Chance in hopes that a female could connect with the motherless child the counselor identified as in need of help. It didn't appear to be working.

Rainey stood and walked to the kitchen counter. She topped off her cup with fresh brew from the half empty pot warming on the coffee maker and looked out the window toward the garage. The snow fell heavier now. The grayness of the day delayed the sunrise. The glass in the garage's oversized rolling doors glowed with the stark white light of the fluorescent tubes illuminating the interior. As Rainey turned back to Chance, she noticed on the counter a picture of the sheepishly smiling teenager standing beside his pride and joy.

"The paint on this truck looks exactly like the original. That shade of green is hard to come by."

Chance opened his eyes to see Rainey holding the framed picture in her hand. He didn't say anything, but at least she had his attention.

She continued, "You did a great job on the woodwork. All hand-sanded and stained, I bet." Softening her features and smiling not at him, but the photo, Rainey asked, "Did you do a wood floor in the bed too? I can't tell from this picture."

"Yes."

Finally, she had drawn out a responsive syllable, and a whole word at that. Rainey leaped at the opening.

"What's under the hood, restored original or custom?"

"Cust—"

That was the last syllable Chance Hale spoke before the wall behind Rainey buckled with an explosive concussion. She noticed a split second of total silence, as if the sound was too loud to hear, then came the blast that sent her diving for the floor. The picture frame and coffee cup flew from her hands. The shattered windows showered the room with tiny shards of glass. Wood splintered into skin ripping projectiles.

Rainey lay stunned on the floor, her ears ringing. As the air and disorientation began to clear, her instincts kicked in. She pushed herself up from the floor, grabbed the Glock from her waist, and went immediately into a defensive posture. She had no idea what had just happened, but it couldn't be a good sign that snow mixed with bits of insulation floated into the kitchen through the gaping hole in the wall.

She called out to Chance, who was under the table, "Are you okay? Are you hurt?"

Chance's eyes were focused on a hubcap that spun like a top not two feet from the now wide-awake teenager. Rainey thought he might be thinking about how close it had come to taking his head off. A small secondary explosion made them both flinch.

Warily watching the door leading to the back porch for a foe and hoping for a friend, she tried again for a response. "Are you hurt? What the hell just happened?"

Rainey saw the hatred in his eyes when Chance responded, not with concern for his father, but with absolute abhorrence.

"That fucker blew up my truck."

Rainey was still a bit disoriented she thought. Maybe she didn't hear him correctly.

She asked one more time, "Are you hurt?"

Chance answered with a question. "If he isn't dead, will you kill him?"

"Not unless I have to," she said, moving her eyes from the door to the teenager.

"If I told you he was a killer, would it make a difference?"

Rainey glanced at the door and then back to Chance, before she answered, "No. I can't just execute him."

He gave Rainey a cold stare and declared, "I can."

#

Later that morning...
U.S. Border Patrol Office
Pembina, North Dakota

Rainey stood in the hallway, tilting her head from side to side. The volume of the constant ear-ringing increased and receded with the movement of her head. She had shaken much of the rubble dust from her thick curls and washed her face at the scene with water from a bottle offered by a paramedic. He had then carefully touched an antibiotic ointment covered cotton swab to the tiny lacerations peppering the parts of Rainey's skin exposed to splintering debris during the blast.

After a few minutes of repeated painful prodding, she had pushed his hand away and said, "Enough with the poking." Apparently, the tone of her voice encouraged her early release from care.

Less than three miles from the Canadian border, the closest federal law enforcement office to the Hale home belonged to the US Border Patrol in downtown Pembina, North Dakota. After giving her statement to the investigating agents from the Bureau's district field office, the agents from Alcohol, Tobacco, and Firearms (ATF), the local agencies, and the state patrol, Rainey had been asked to wait at the Border Patrol office. Before she left, evidence discovered at the scene suggested Joshua Lee Hale was, as his son had claimed, a murderer. Crime scene gossip said behavioral analysts were on the way from Quantico.

Rainey was happy to leave the chaotic scene for several reasons. One, she needed time and somewhere quiet to think. Secondly, Supervisory Special Agent Hébert had been well respected and deeply loved by his colleagues across the various law enforcement departments in the area. As each arrived on the scene, their eyes questioned her with looks that implied Hébert would not be dead had one of them accompanied him to the Hale house.

The investigation would find her blameless. She had followed her supervisor's directive and remained with Chance Hale inside the home. A serial murderer took Hébert's life. A wife lost her husband, children lost a father, grandchildren lost their Papa, the FBI lost an agent, and the people giving her strange looks had lost a friend. She didn't resent their suspicion, but she was happy to be away from their mournful contemplations.

11

She peered through the tiny window of the interrogation room door at the most compelling reason to leave the crime scene. Sitting on the floor in the corner, head resting against the wall, and still covered in dust from the explosion, Chance Hale slept off his hangover. Rainey had not forced him to stay in the room. He asked to be placed there so he could "just be left alone."

A border patrol officer, wearing a nametag that read Santee, said, "I'm sorry about your partner," as he handed Rainey a steaming mug of coffee.

"Thank you for the coffee," she said, and then explained, "Hébert was my temporary supervisor, a good man who will be missed. I've only known him about a week, but I really liked him. In hindsight, we shouldn't have split up."

Officer Santee pointed out, "Then you'd be dead too."

"I suppose so. Still, somebody must be blamed, right?"

"I know what you mean. The higher-ups are going to want to know how he came across the border with all those women."

"I'm sure they will," Rainey answered, a bit distracted by her own thoughts.

"From what the crime scene techs found in his bedroom, they believe Joshua Lee Hale has been crossing the border with First Nations women from Winnipeg for seven years—one about every three or four months since he moved here from North Carolina."

Rainey stared at the sleeping teen on the other side of the door.

Santee continued his monologue. "John Joe, uh, he's with the state lab, he said there were trucking-style logs back to 1991 detailing each victim's abduction—like he was picking up and tracking a load or something. He said it looked like Hale thought of it as shipping women down to Texas and Mexico. Good thing he wrote their names down, or we would have never known who they were. They're bones by now, in a desert somewhere, I suppose."

Rainey sipped her coffee and watched Chance Hale's chest slowly rise and fall with his steady breathing.

Santee leaned closer to look into the window. "You ever see a kid sleep like that after seeing his dad blow himself up?"

"He didn't really see it. But no, I haven't seen a child react this way to witnessing a parent's violent death. Then again, people's reactions to trauma are never predictable. Of course, since he apparently hated his father enough to want him dead, this might be the first time he's had a decent sleep in a long time."

"I hadn't thought about that," Santee said.

"He is also hung over and reeks of alcohol and pot. He could just be sleeping off last night's indulgence." She looked away from the window and turned to Santee. "Do you think we could get him something to eat? He might be more attentive with some warm food in his body."

Santee was already moving away when he said, "I'll be right back. The diner on the corner makes a great cheeseburger. Perfect for a hangover."

"Sounds like the voice of experience," Rainey called after him.

"He's not the first interviewee needing some grease to coat his gut," the patrol officer said, as he grabbed the knob of the door leading out to the main hallway. "Can I bring you something, too Agent Bell?"

Rainey raised the coffee mug in Santee's direction. "I'm good. Thank you."

Rainey returned to staring through the little window and to wondering if the recently orphaned Chance Obadiah Hale was, in fact, the murdering son of a serial killer. She had not mentioned to Santee that in her experience most people who slept in an interrogation room were guilty of something. Alyson Grayson was still missing, and Rainey believed Chance knew where she was.

"You should not have said that."

Rainey heard Hébert's voice lingering in her head. He had chastised her after they met with Alyson's parents.

"Should not have said what?" Rainey had asked him.

"You promised Mrs. Grayson we would find her daughter and the man who took her. First, you don't know it was a man or that she was taken. Second, you don't know we'll find him or her. We don't know who those victims are from the lake. Do you think some investigator told their parents they would find them and catch their killers?" He paused, but he really didn't want an answer. He sent the message home with his next words. "Don't promise heartbroken people things you can't deliver. What you can promise is that we will pursue the case until we find answers and we will not stop. That, I can promise Alyson's mother."

Rainey's only response option had been, "Yes, sir."

Even with his warning, Hébert had believed Chance Hale had something to do with Alyson Grayson's disappearance. Rainey agreed and vowed silently to prove it one day. She watched Chance's chest rise and fall for a full minute. Assured he was sleeping deeply, she sat down in a chair just outside the door. She pulled out her notepad and started reviewing Alyson's case from the beginning.

#

"Chance, may I sit with you?"

Rainey closed the door and crossed the interrogation room to the table where Chance devoured the last bites of the cheeseburger Santee had delivered a few minutes ago.

13

Chance swallowed. Squinted up at her and burped out two syllables, "Law-yer."

"Wow, such talent, and two syllables in a row. We're nearly having a conversation now."

Rainey smiled and pulled out a chair. She sat across from him and flopped her notepad open on the table, exposing info she had on Alyson Grayson's case that implicated Chance—tire tracks to his door, names of witnesses who saw them leave together, Alyson's fingerprints on the garage door and his restored Chevy—all proof she had been with him the night she disappeared. He had never denied Alyson gave him a ride home, but Chance claimed no memory once they arrived outside the Hale garage, where the ATV had been parked under the lean-to shelter, leaving behind wet tire tracks still visible on the concrete the next morning when her father came looking.

Chance glanced at the notes and reiterated, "Law—"

Rainey waved her hand to stop his rebuff. She couldn't talk to him about the case, but she could watch him while he watched her.

"I know, I know. 'Law-yer.' I'm not asking you questions about any crimes you may have witnessed or participated in. You have invoked your right to counsel, so no questions about Alyson or frozen bodies or your dad's apparent crimes. I'm just here to keep you company. How was the cheeseburger?"

Chance tossed the last bite into his mouth, smacked his lips loudly throughout the mastication process, and stared back at her with contempt. Without looking down, he flipped her notebook shut with the index finger on his left hand and intensified his sneering glare as he swallowed. Rainey pretended not to notice his tough guy routine.

"Were the fries good? They looked good. I think there isn't a better taste in the world than a good French fry dipped in thick ketchup. You know, if I ever have to pick a last meal, it's going to have French fries and ketchup, maybe a double order. What would you order for a last meal?"

Santee had delivered a supersized soda with the food. He said he figured the kid was probably dehydrated. Chance reached for the drink, rattled the ice around in the empty Styrofoam cup, and then proceeded to make dry sucking noises until he tired of his cleverness.

"Well, I'll be sure to get a big soda when I order the fries. Sounds like you enjoyed it as much as the burger."

Rainey hoped the sarcasm wasn't lost on Chance and doubted that it was, as she met his glare. The stare-off ended seconds later when, after a quick knock, Border Agent Santee entered the room escorting the tall redhead Rainey and Hébert encountered at the Hale home earlier.

Santee said as he entered, "Here he is ma'am. Safe, sound, and well fed."

14

Fully awake now and dressed for the weather, Jean Berry's deeply crimson hair made her head appear to glow inside the white fur-lined parka she wore. Rainey had guessed her to be in her mid-forties when they first met, but fully dolled up and coiffed, she appeared to fit more in the mid to late thirties range. Even as she gave the impression of a much younger woman, Jean Berry's look was pure 1930s soundstage starlet. She had painted highly arched brows over darkly lined and long-lashed eyes. Her poisoned apple red tinted full lips of a starlet from the golden era of Hollywood pursed into a smile. The style was so out of place, it was startling but expertly done.

She pushed past Santee and with a hand extended in Rainey's direction said, "Hello, I'm Jean Berry. You were at the house this morning, weren't you? I'm sorry, with all the drama of the day, I don't recall your name."

Rainey noted Jean's discourteous attitude from the morning had been replaced with the "nice" woman Hébert had described.

Taking the offered hand, she answered, "Special Agent Bell, FBI, ma'am. I'm glad you were not injured in the explosion."

"As it turns out, that is a well-built old house. Thank goodness. I seem to have faired better than you. Keep ointment on those little cuts, so you don't scar, dear." She glanced at Chance and then returned her attention to Rainey. "This has all been so upsetting. Thank you for looking after our boy until I could come for him."

"I'm sorry, ma'am. I don't recall learning your relationship to Chance."

The redhead left Rainey and strode quickly to Chance's side. She hugged his head to her breast and cooed to him, "I'm so sorry hon. I'm so sorry about all this."

Chance seemed taken aback by the affection, but relaxed into a smile, he aimed at Rainey. His rescue was underway, and he knew it.

Jean bent to his ear and whispered something, before turning to respond to Rainey's inquiry. She pulled away, looked Chance in the eyes, and waited for his confused but acquiescent nod in agreement to whatever she had said. Her manner remained friendly, but her tone took on a more serious air.

"I work for Hale trucking, and I'm a friend of the family. I've known this child since the day he was born. Is he being detained?"

Rainey watched the smirk form on Chance's lips.

"No, ma'am. Chance is not being detained, nor has he been questioned. He asked for a lawyer."

Jean Berry reached into her oversized purse for a small card case. She retrieved a card and held it out to Rainey.

"The Hale family's attorney is Horace Blackman out of Durham, North Carolina, but he has representation here as well. If you have further questions for Chance, please contact Mr. Blackman's office."

Rainey knew the agents on the scene were coming to speak with Chance. Even if he had asked for a lawyer, she knew she would catch hell for letting him go. She attempted an end around. Jean Berry had said she was a friend, not a relative.

"Ms. Berry, you understand I can't release a juvenile to a non-family member without some notice from the next of kin."

"Well, aren't you on top of things? I wouldn't have it any other way," Jean said, with more drawl than she had exhibited before, a sure sign of victory in Rainey's experience.

Jean reached back into the cavernous purse and produced a document, which she handed to Rainey.

"Chance's grandfather, OB, is his legal guardian. That's a faxed document giving me authority to represent him in this matter. The original is on the way as we speak."

Rainey examined the document. It was exactly what Jean Berry purported it to be.

The older woman patted Rainey's arm, interrupting her perusal, saying, "You're so sweet to make sure he's with the right people. I truly appreciate your concern."

With that declaration, Jean gathered up Chance and marched him out the door. The two appeared to have practiced the exodus. Although much of his juvenile record was sealed, rumors and this display of behavior indicated this wasn't Chance's first interrogation room exit accompanied by Jean or some other family representative. If Rainey wasn't positive of this assessment, the slightly demonic sneer of victory Chance gave her on the way out sealed the deal.

Rainey called out to him, "Hey, Chance. I'll be seeing you."

3

April 6, 1998
Behavioral Science Unit
FBI Training Division
Quantico, Virginia

Escorted to the open office doorway of Supervisory Special Agent Robert Douglas Wood for her scheduled appointment, Rainey was told to wait there until called. She shifted her weight from foot to foot. Her hands went into her pockets and out again. She checked her watch repeatedly. She tugged at her suit jacket, picked lint from her sleeve, and generally fidgeted for nearly four full minutes.

SSA Wood finally acknowledged her presence with a gravelly, "Come in."

He pointed to a chair facing his desk without losing focus on the file folder lying open in front of him. Rainey noted the citations and awards on the walls while she waited for his attention. This was it—the holy grail of her career dreams. Seated across from the man who would determine her suitability for a coveted spot in the Behavioral Science training program, she could barely contain the smile threatening to burst forth.

Without looking up from his reading, SSA Wood picked up a pen to make a note and simultaneously asked, "So, Bell, would you like to explain why you have continued to investigate a case that both the locals and your supervisors have deemed closed?"

Rainey saw her dream job slipping from her grasp. When the order came to report to Quantico for an interview, it had been a surprise. She had made it clear that assignment to the newly renamed Behavioral

Analysis Unit was her career goal, but Rainey's four years of experience as a field agent were short of the bare minimum for consideration. She estimated she would be in ten years before they looked at her application. With the tone of SSA Wood's first question, it looked like it might be much longer, if ever.

Wood looked up from his desk. He took off his reading glasses and used one of the earpieces as a pointer, putting Rainey squarely on the spot.

"Well, spit it out. If it was worth risking yet another insubordination letter in your jacket, then let's hear it."

Seizing the opportunity offered her; Rainey began to explain, "Sir, I continued to look for Alyson Grayson, because I don't believe Joshua Lee Hale had anything to do with her disappearance."

Rainey paused for her superior's reaction, which came bluntly.

"Belief and evidence are not held in the same light in a court of law." Wood motioned again with his glasses for Rainey to continue. "Tell me— on what evidence do you base your belief?"

"Joshua Lee Hale's victims were not well-kept teenage girls. He took women no one would miss right away, if at all—homeless women, some prostitutes, a few drug addicts, and as far as we can tell mostly First Nations women looking for a way into the states from Winnipeg. Hale made no record of any victims outside of that profile. His logbook said he was in Canada when Alyson disappeared. That is verified by the shipping dock where he picked up his load, and we have video evidence of his actual border crossing."

Wood placed his elbows on the desk and leaned forward. Rainey had dreamed of exchanges like this since the first time she attended one of SSA Wood's Academy lectures. She was just one of many agents he couldn't possibly remember, but she had never forgotten. Rainey listened intently as Wood attempted to poke holes in her theory.

"It has been suggested Hale crossed the border without his truck. That maybe he had a planted vehicle on the Canadian side and returned to get his truck later. How does that sit with your theory?" Wood asked.

Rainey countered with a question of her own. "Why go to all that trouble for the neighbor girl he could have grabbed anytime?"

"But it is possible," Wood added.

"Yes, sir, but the two girls in the lake behind Hale's house—he had nothing about them in his meticulously kept logbooks. Joshua Hale recorded the interactions he had with every woman he carried down to Mexico. Yet, not one word about the teenagers in the lake. I find that odd."

Wood nodded in agreement. "Yes, that is an anomaly. Go on."

Rainey suppressed the smile and continued, "He hauled the CANAMEX corridor from Mexico City to Winnipeg. One of the victims found in the lake, Adeline Tuttle, was a college student from Greensboro, North Carolina, who went missing June 7, 1996. Greensboro is very near Hale Trucking's home base, but nowhere near where Joshua Hale abducted his victims. He never hunted in North Carolina, according to his logbooks. The logbooks don't even start until after he moved to North Dakota."

"Murderers lie, Bell."

"Yes, sir, but there are these trucker's knots used to tie the lake victims, more ritualistic than necessary. The bodies were frozen and then placed in the lake, a more unique disposal method than 'delivery to Mexico' as Hale described in his notes. Also, the lake victims went missing between June of 1996 and December of 1997. Hale started logging his victims in 1991. According to Hale's porn collection, he has some fetish preferences, but he isn't into rope ritual."

Wood suggested an alternative to her theory. "These guys don't always follow a pattern. They adapt. Maybe he got bored and wanted something new."

Rainey had known she would have to support her assertions if she ever made her investigation known. She had made the mistake of presenting her findings to her current supervisor, and now here she was defending her investigative instincts. Rainey had prepared for Wood's skepticism. She took a deep breath and began.

"I didn't just check his log books. I also checked his company shipping records. He couldn't have been the person who took the other girl in the lake, Inge Abrahamsen. She was from Minneapolis and according to her mother went missing on March 14, 1997. Unless she ran away—like the police first thought—and wasn't abducted until a few days after her mother reported her missing, Joshua Hale could not have taken her."

Wood interrupted, "But again, it is possible she did run away and was abducted when Hale could have been the perp."

"Yes, sir, but hear me out. We don't know what Hale's signature was. We haven't found a trace of his victims. The killer of the teen girls definitely has a signature—the head injury, the knots, and the freezing. It's important to him."

One corner of Wood's mouth curled into a slight smile. "I'm sure it is."

Rainey, excited at Wood's apparent approval, hurried the remaining portion of her defense.

"I discovered two other murdered teenagers who met the victim profile. Madison Parker, age fifteen, disappeared from Burke, Wisconsin on December 21, 1996, and was found in Sinclair Lewis Park in Minnesota thirteen days later. Sharon Long, age sixteen, went missing from the same Sinclair Lewis Park on July 3, 1997, and found frozen, well really, she was melting in a field in North Dakota one month later. Both of these cases fit in the time frame, both had the same trucker's knot binding their wrists and ankles, both were frozen. Madison Parker was taken and found in winter, so no one thought anything of her frozen condition, but finding the frozen body of Sharon Long in mid-summer drew the investigators' attention to truckers driving freezer rigs. The trucker's knot and the connected locations may be circumstantial, but my dad taught me there are no coincidences, only unseen connections."

"Your dad is a smart man," Wood remarked.

Rainey barely paused for Wood's comment before adding, "All of these girls matched Alyson Grayson's physical appearance, blonde, blue eyes, slender athletic build, and—"

Wood's hand went up in a "Stop" motion.

"Okay, okay, you sold me," he said. "You did all this research on your own time, I take it."

"Yes, sir. I made a lot of phone inquiries. My dad lives outside of Raleigh. The last few months, on my trips home from North Dakota, I drove the route and talked to law enforcement with missing teens fitting the profile. I could only find the additional two, but there could be more."

Wood challenged Rainey with, "If these are not victims of Joshua Hale, then who?"

"There is one other thing about all these victims, sir. Each went missing while school was out, either over the summer or one of the shorter vacation periods. I believe someone else with Hale Trucking is also a serial murderer, and I believe Chance Hale knows who it is and/or is involved in some way. In either case, I'm positive he knows something about Alyson Grayson's disappearance."

Wood leaned back in his chair. Rainey focused on how he slowly tapped the earpiece of his glasses on his bottom lip while contemplating her proposal.

Wood finally commented, "That's a hell of a reach—two serial murderers working for one company."

"I know, but I believe this whole thing is a family affair. I just have no idea how to prove it. If Chance's silence about his father's murders is any indication, loyalty is deeply ingrained in the Hale clan."

"The family that kills together stays together, eh?"

Rainey nodded her head. "Sir, I don't believe the Bloody Benders killed as many as this family has. And what makes it worse is I don't think they are finished."

4

"Tammy, may I come in?"

Tammy Lynn Gaskill brought her blue and bloodshot eyes up to meet the compassionate, deep brown eyes of the speaker. Permission to enter came in the form of a quivering nod from the patient in trauma bed three.

"Tammy, I am Deputy Robertson with the Durham County Sheriff's Office. You can call me Sheila if that makes you more comfortable."

Another silent nod from Tammy told the deputy she could continue.

"Tammy, I'm going to ask you a few questions. Is that all right?"

A dry, "Yes," came from the bed. A cough followed, and then another.

Deputy Robertson reached for the glass of water on the tray table and handed it to the trembling young teen.

"Here, take a few sips. It'll help. It's always so dry in the hospital."

Tammy drank as if she had just emerged from wandering the desert. She handed the empty glass back to the deputy and spoke clearly for the first time.

"I can't seem to get enough water."

Deputy Robertson refilled the glass and gave it back to Tammy.

"You drink as much as you need. It will help flush the drugs from your system."

Tammy drank again, while the deputy asked, "I'm told you just turned fourteen. Is that right? You can just nod if you want."

Tammy nodded and added a "Yes" between sips.

"You attend Hillsborough Middle School, correct?"

Tammy put the glass down on the tray table and answered, "I'm in eighth grade," before pulling the covers up under her chin. "I'm just so cold."

Deputy Robertson stuck her notepad in her jacket pocket, before reaching for the folded blanket on the end of the bed.

"Here, let's cover you with this," she said and tucked the blanket around Tammy as if she were a child of her own. "How's that? Better?"

"Yes, thank you, Depu— Uh, Sheila."

"Good. Now, Tammy, I'd like to hear your version of last night's events. I talked with the deputies who brought you here and your doctors and nurses. I know you have been through a lot, and I apologize for having to ask some of the same questions you have already answered. I'm trying to find out what happened to you."

The previously meek teenager became animated, nearly shouting, "I don't know what happened. I don't know how I got there. I don't know where my clothes are. I can't believe this is happening."

Deputy Robertson relied on her recent Sexual Assault Response Team or SART training to offer support.

"Tammy, you take all the time you need to be angry, to be sad, to be afraid, and back to angry again. You feel any way you feel. No one can know how this will affect you and you will have to process this trauma in the unique way that will work for you."

Tammy sobbed softly.

The deputy continued. "I hope that you will take advantage of the help that will be offered you. There is no one-size fits all treatment for sexual assault, but one thing is always absolutely clear. The victim is never at fault. You are not responsible for what happened to you. I need you to acknowledge that you hear me."

Tammy nodded and took the tissue Deputy Robertson offered her.

"Are you able to continue answering questions?"

Tammy took a deep breath and let it out slowly, before answering, "Yes."

"Okay. What is the last thing you remember?"

"I was at the river with friends."

"The Eno River?"

"Yes, near Few's Ford."

Deputy Robertson wrote the info down.

"Were there a lot of people? Do you know the names of everyone that was there?"

Tammy shook her head. "I knew most of them, but there were people from all over. You know, just kids from around."

22

"Do you remember how you got separated from the rest of the group?"

Tammy shook her head, indicating she could not recall.

"Can you tell me what else you remember?"

Tammy searched her memory, taking a moment before she answered, "I remember the sun starting to go down, music, and laughing. I remember the smell of the fire pit. Then I see flashes of dark woods. I just kept walking. I was so cold. I remember being naked on the golf course when the cops found me. That's it."

Deputy Robertson finished writing a note on her pad and then asked, "Can you give me the names of a few people I could talk to? Maybe they can fill in some of the blanks."

Tammy listed two names. "Jennifer Gables and Emily Santini. My mom has their phone numbers. She makes me give her all my friend's numbers."

"That's a smart mom you have. I'll get that info from her. Anything else you think I need to know?"

Tammy thought for a second. "I don't know. I mean, I can't really say for sure."

Deputy Robertson was intrigued. "Tell me what it is. We never know what little thing will solve a case."

"I think I saw Chance Hale. We were friends before he moved to North Dakota. He's two years older than me, but I always kind of liked him.

"And you think you saw this Chance Hale last night?"

"I believe he was there. It might have been his cousin Robby. I don't know why I keep thinking about him. I know he wouldn't hurt me. He was always nice to me. Like kid sister nice, you know."

"Okay, anyone else?"

"I...I can't remember."

Tammy started to sob, indicating she needed another break from the constant questioning she had endured since being found wandering naked on a golf course at sunrise. The emergency room staff and the trained sexual assault team reported Tammy had been raped, multiple times and in every way possible. She showed no visible signs of being beaten or restrained, but she did have bruising from being handled roughly. Evidence of rape was irrefutable according to the ER doctor who treated her. She needed stitches to repair tearing. He was sure she had been drugged but had to wait for the toxicology report to know what was in her system. It was definitely a dissociative anesthetic. Tammy Gaskill might never remember what happened to her.

"You get some rest, and I'll come see you again before I go."

Deputy Robertson stepped into the hallway where her colleagues waited.

"She named him too, just like the other kids did. Her parents suspect him, as well. Whoever this kid is, everyone thinks he's capable of this crime."

A deputy wearing an Orange County Sheriff's Department uniform spoke up, "I know this guy. He was accused of sexual assault a few years back. Rumors say his grandfather got the charges dropped—paid off the girl's father. Chance left town right after we questioned him. He went to live with his dad in North Dakota."

Deputy Robertson started nodding with sudden recognition of the name, before she said, "Hale. His dad was a serial killer, right?"

The Orange County deputy replied, "Yep. Joshua Lee Hale. He blew himself and an FBI agent sky high last January. Like father like son, I guess."

Deputy Robertson looked back at the trauma room door where Tammy Gaskill waited inside to begin the process of healing.

"For that young woman's sake," she said, "we can only hope it's that simple. It rarely is."

5

"Frank 25. Dispatch. In pursuit of suspect. On foot in the fenced area behind Hale Trucking."

"Dispatch. Frank 25 out of the car and in foot pursuit. Do you need backup?"

"Frank 25. Dispatch. That's a negative at this time."

"Dispatch. Frank 25. Roger that."

Orange County Deputy Kendal Kemble replaced the radio on his hip. He walked out of the gate at the back of the Hale Trucking parking lot and entered the woods. His assigned rookie for the evening followed behind.

"Man, this woods is thick, ain't it?"

Kemble corrected the fresh-faced rookie's grammar. "Isn't it?"

"Yeah, it is. What makes you think we're going to catch him in here anyway? He'll have to come back out to the road. It's a ways to the highway and there ain't nothin' else out here."

"There isn't anything."

"Then why are we—"

Kemble cut him off with, "Shut up, will you, Tucker? This is your first time on nights, and it's Halloween. You should maybe think about listening and not running your mouth nonstop. All right?"

"Okay, sure. I just don't see why we got to come all the way out here, in the dark, at nearly three in the morning. We got his car, his wallet, and his keys."

"We would have him if you had been paying attention while I ran his information," Kemble said.

"He started puking again. I didn't want him to puke on my shoes. He looked too sick to ru—"

Deputy Kemble cut Tucker's chatter off when he dropped to one knee and raised a closed fist in the air. Faintly, just out of his flashlight's reach he heard a twig snap and then another, in rapid succession and some distance apart. Whoever it was moved fast, taking long strides. Only a person familiar with the area could run through this forest in the dark with that much confidence.

As Kemble tracked the footfalls, Tucker raised his weapon and shouted, "Stop! Police!"

"Do not fire that weapon, rookie," Kemble said. "He's just a kid."

Tucker challenged the reprimand. "It's probably a deer anyway."

"Deer don't generally jangle keys as they run," Kemble said, as he rose from his crouched position. "Come on. He's headed toward the old grotto."

"The old what?"

"It's like a manmade cave. Old man Hale used to keep a pet lion out here. The lion died in the eighties. It's been grown over for years. Kids party in the grotto sometimes, especially since the old man's grandkids became teenagers."

Tucker followed Kemble through the trees. He asked, "Isn't there another way in here? Like maybe a way to drive up in the car with the big lights strapped to it."

"Now where is the fun in that?" Kemble replied with a chuckle. "No, we can't drive to it. The old man put up an eight-foot chain link fence topped with razor wire on this property. That gate back there is the only way in or out. We searched for evidence on this property when old man Hale's son, Joshua, turned out to be a serial killer. The State and FBI lab guys were all over this place."

"Did ya' find any bodies or parts?" Tucker asked with a morbid excitement that rubbed Kemble the wrong way.

"No, we didn't. Jesus, do you ever shut up?"

Kemble pushed through the trees, leaving Tucker in a wake of branches snapping back into place. After a few more yards, his flashlight beam fell on the thick Carolina Jessamine vines that obscured the chain link fence surrounding the old grotto. He walked around the corner to see the gate standing open. He heard Tucker trip over a root and stumble around behind him.

At the same time, someone began heaving. The sound of projectile vomiting on the concrete floor inside followed. Kemble peeked into the darkness beyond the gate. The beam of his flashlight lit up a teenager on his knees engaged in vomiting over a ledge into the dark abyss formed by the sunken area where a lion had once lived. The grotto looked like a forgotten zoo exhibit, overgrown and eerily quiet, except for the puking teenager.

"Don't bother getting up right now, but when you're done, I need to see you out here," Kemble said to the teen, who glanced over at the light before returning to the task at hand.

"That ain't him," Tucker said, as he regained his balance and joined Kemble at the gate.

"It isn't him," Kemble corrected.

"That's what I said. Where'd the other guy go?" Tucker asked the puking young man.

The response was more retching.

Kemble stepped through the gate and aimed his light around. Beer cans and broken liquor bottles tumbled out of an overflowing fifty-gallon drum near the gate. He felt a near carpet of smashed cigarette butts under his feet. On the floor between two old truck seats, a stack of well-worn porn magazines stuck together from the humidity and dampness trapped inside the vine-covered grotto.

Along with the seats, a discarded couch, with five wooden legs and a brick substituted for a missing sixth, formed a circle around a halved steel drum with a dying fire inside. The couch held a second young man passed out in a sleeping bag with a mostly empty bottle of whiskey still clutched in his hand. An empty sleeping bag lay stretched across two seats that had been pushed together. Kemble surmised it belonged to the kid a few feet away, the one trying to keep his guts from coming out his mouth. Neither of the inebriated occupants of the grotto was the young man Kemble and Tucker had chased into the woods.

Kemble approached the puking teenager, who was at least conscious. "Hey, what's your name?

The teen turned to face Kemble, still on all fours. He wiped his mouth with the sleeve of his hoodie and answered, "Robby Hughes."

Tucker, who was suddenly at Kemble's shoulder, said, "That's the name of the guy we're chasing, but this ain't him."

Kemble ignored Tucker. "I need to see some ID."

The teen's coloring had left his face. He was too sick to lie. He answered, "I left my wallet in the car."

"Where's your car?"

"Up at the house."

"Are you Roger Hughes boy?"

"Yes, sir."

"Who is that?" Kemble asked while aiming his flashlight at the passed-out teen on the couch.

"My cousin, Chance."

Kemble knew neither of these kids was the one they found puking on the side of the road. He was about to ask the real Robby Hughes if he knew who might be driving his car at this hour. They were interrupted by the sound wave that came a half a second before the night sky erupted with an explosion that shook the ground. The concussion rumbled through the cavernous grotto. The concrete forming the cave-like structure coughed dust into the air. The metal bars creaked against the steel mesh that covered the open-air roof, raining rust and dirt down on the occupants.

"Holy shit," Tucker said and hit the ground like a veteran fresh from the combat zone, which he was. "That was close, man. Somebody's blowing shit up out here. Big shit!"

Kemble had served during Operation Desert Shield. He had heard his share of explosions. That was indeed a large one. The flash had penetrated the heavy vegetation covering the grotto, but he could see nothing through it now. He stepped outside and peered through the dense woods. Over the tops of the trees, the reflection of fire glowed orange on fingers of smoke spiraling upward. Pieces of insulation and particles of debris floated down like snowflakes in the beam of his flashlight.

"Frank 25 to Dispatch," Kemble said into his radio.

"Frank 25, go ahead."

"Dispatch, you're going to want to roll fire and ambulances, detectives, bomb squad…oh hell, just send everybody. That boom I'm sure you heard was Hale Trucking blowing sky high."

#

"The Dread Pirate Roberts?"

"Yeah, he was dressed like the Dread Pirate Roberts. You know, like from the 'Princess Bride' movie."

"I know who the Dread Pirate Roberts is. You're telling me the guy that was puking on the side of the road when you pulled up was dressed like the Dread—"

Tucker interrupted the detective. "—Pirate Roberts. Head covered in black, black pants, shoes, shirt, you know."

The detective asked, "Did he have a cape, a mask?"

"No on the cape, but yeah, he had a mask pushed up on his forehead."

The detective seemed relieved to see Kemble walking toward him.

"Hey, Kemble," he said, beckoning him closer. "Describe the guy you were chasing."

"Five feet ten inches tall, about a hundred and fifty pounds, Caucasian, looked and sounded like a teenager, light hair color, blond probably, pulled back in a ponytail. Black pants, black athletic shoes, black turtleneck under a black hoodie, black knit hat with eye and nose holes worn pushed up on his forehead."

The detective looked at Tucker. Sarcasm smothered his question, "Dread Pirate Roberts?" He looked back to Kemble, "Where do you get these guys?"

Kemble shrugged. "He can shoot the eyes out of a gnat at a thousand yards and disarm an IED with his eyes closed, so we'll work on the rest."

The detective's attitude changed a bit, but not much. "Okay then, you tell me what happened."

"We came up on a car pulled over on the shoulder and saw an individual vomiting in the grass. We stopped. He didn't appear to be under the influence. He said he just felt sick and pulled over, but he was too jumpy to be innocent. I went back to the cruiser to run his info when he decided to bolt. As it turns out, neither the car nor the ID was his. While we were searching for the guy that ran, we found two of OB Hale's grandsons drunk in the old grotto, Chance Hale passed out and Robby Hughes too sick to stand. We had just ascertained that the car and ID given to us by the suspect we were chasing belonged to Robby when the explosion happened. I thought one of the fuel tanks blew at the trucking office."

"Unfortunately," the detective said, looking at the smoldering ruins of a large structure, "it was the house that blew up. Fire says it was probably a propane leak."

Firefighters picked through the debris, in search of live embers. One knelt then raised his head so that his voice carried clearly, when he said, "I've got human remains here."

6

February 16, 2000
Federal Bureau of Investigation
National Center for the Analysis of Violent Crime
Quantico, Virginia

"Bell! Hey, Bell, wait up."

Rainey didn't look back.

She called over her shoulder, "What is it, McNally? Still trying to figure out how not to pay off on that bet?"

"No, no, you'll get your fancy bottle of whiskey."

"Tequila," Rainey corrected him, as she continued around the track.

"Yeah, yeah, I wrote it down."

Special Agent Danny McNally was the exact opposite of what people thought of when picturing an FBI agent. Far from dark and severe, Danny's freckled cherub cheeks reflected his Irish roots and seemed always to frame a smile. His head full of red wavy hair sat atop his tall and broad frame. McNally had been in Rainey's academy class. It was her acceptance to the BSU training program before him that cost Agent McNally a nice bottle of Don Julio Real, even if she was ahead of him by only a few months.

McNally began to breathe harder as he quickened his pace to come alongside her. Rainey could hear him gaining ground and lengthened her stride.

"Come on, Rainey, wait up. It's important. Wood sent me."

Rainey eased to a cool-down lap pace.

Danny fell into stride with her. "Thank you for slowing down," he said, a bit out of breath. "I'm not out of shape, but I'm the guy you hounds run the fox to. I'll tackle them, but I won't ever catch a runner."

"It's important to know your strengths," Rainey said, patting him on the back and laughing. It was then she noticed he was in street clothes. "Not a bad pace for dress shoes, though."

"I didn't have time to change. The old man said go find you. So I did."

The old man was SSA Robert Douglas Wood. He recommended her for the behavioral science training program and taught a few classes she attended, but Rainey had not been called in for an office conference since that first interview. She couldn't imagine what he wanted. Unless it was time to find out what her future was going to look like.

"Is Wood making the placements today? I thought the decisions would come down next week."

She jogged to a stop by her gym bag and reached for the water bottle inside.

Danny seemed thankful when Rainey stopped moving.

He kicked off a dress shoe and rubbed his arch, "I'm rethinking my opposition to rubber-soled dress shoes."

"Try Rockports," she said, before asking again, "What does Wood want?"

Danny looked up from examining his foot. "I walked by his office and he yelled at me to go find you, ASAP."

"It's probably because I was talking to O'Toole about a school shooter inquiry from one of my dad's war buddies, Wellman Wise. Remember him from the academy computer class I helped teach. He asked my dad to arrange a meeting. He wanted to talk about a possible school shooter thing. I guess the old boys were testing me."

"It could be Wood needs to see you and not some conspiracy theory," Danny said, adding, "You're paranoid, Bell."

"I don't believe in coincidence," Rainey countered, as she removed her damp sweatshirt. She stood in the crisp air in only her sports bra and corrected Danny's appraisal of her. "I'm prepared, not paranoid. There is a difference."

"You aren't modest either," Danny observed.

"It's a sports bra." Rainey indicated the other runners, mostly men, with a nod of her head, adding, "These guys have seen more at the beach."

Cool and dry, she retrieved a clean academy tee shirt and FBI windbreaker from her bag and redressed. She thanked Danny for finding her, tossed him her water bottle, for which he seemed grateful, and then jogged off toward the Behavioral Science section of the academy.

Hoping Wood called her in to give her a BAU assignment, a little voice in the back of her mind chanted, "Not crimes against children. Not crimes against children."

Rainey was at the end of eighteen months of mentored training, which had followed the initial sixteen weeks of additional academy classes. Now among the elite few FBI trained behavioral analysts, she was soon to be assigned to one of the BAU teams. Most recently she had been training with the crimes against children unit. Of all that she had seen, those crimes got down to her bones. Rainey hated cases that involved kids.

She had just completed a preliminary assignment with the crimes against children unit and returned last night from a long-needed vacation in North Carolina with her father. The powers that be would assign her where the bureau thought she would be most effective in the next few days, she'd been told. Rainey assumed she was going to computer crimes because of her computer forensics degree. She also had a graduate degree in behavioral science and hoped that would allow her to work with the crimes against adults unit, the mind hunters.

Rainey felt the most passion for interviewing and researching serial murderers and rapists. Finding out how and why they did it in their own words, learning what they thought caused them to commit the crimes they did, that was the most satisfying part of the job. Of course, she would take whatever assignment the bureau deemed fit and do the job expected of her.

She was telling herself that again when she saw SSA Wood pulling on his coat as he stepped into the hallway.

"Ah, there you are, Bell. Sorry to interrupt your run, but I need you to come with me."

Rainey guessed her workout clothes were a giveaway, but couldn't help the little shiver from imagining Wood as the all seeing eye.

"No problem, sir. I just need a minute to redress."

Wood waved her off. "Do you have your credentials?"

"Yes, sir."

"Then you're dressed."

Rainey fell in step with Wood as he moved off down the hall.

"May I ask where we're going, sir?"

"We're going to see a man about some bones."

#

Ten minutes later...
FBI Laboratory
Quantico, Virginia

"The bones were delivered in this box."

The "man" Wood took Rainey to see turned out to be a woman. While Rainey surveyed the items and evidence bags exhibited on the stainless steel tables in front of her, she listened to senior FBI forensic examiner Dr. Joan Munzer present her findings.

"This is a file storage box. It is very common and distributed widely. The company makes over two million boxes a day. The identifying stamp was removed; so no chance of tracing it. No fingerprints were found on the inside. The outside of the box is covered in the prints of those who processed it through the police department before they realized what it was. Those prints have all been identified and eliminated."

Assuming this was some kind of final test before her unit assignment, Rainey commented, "A pristine box. That doesn't narrow the pool of suspects much. Any office could have a stack of unfolded boxes in the store room."

SSA Wood agreed, "True."

Rainey turned to the woman in the lab coat. "If boxes are found in the suspect's possession, could you match the batch?"

Dr. Munzer nodded her head. "Yes. According to the manufacturer, it would be possible to match batch-mates. I sent a sample of the cardboard to their lab. They may be able to identify approximate date of manufacturing by comparing contents."

Rainey suggested, "A note should be made to include boxes on the search warrant when the time comes."

One corner of SSA Wood's lip curled into a slight smile. He began to fill Rainey in on the case.

"The box was left outside the back entrance of the St. Augustine Dunes Police Department during a rainstorm the night before New Year's Eve. Thinking it was left outside by accident, a clerk brought it in out of the weather. Once they realized what they had, they checked the security cameras. A man in a rain slicker walked out of the shadows, left the box, and disappeared again."

Rainey moved down the table. A short length of jute twine tied in a familiar knot drew her attention. She voiced her realization to Wood, "I suppose this is why I am here."

Dr. Munzer handed over several photos. "These were taken after the box was opened, but before the seal was broken on the bag."

The photos showed the box with the lid removed, exposing a clear, vacuum-sealed bag containing a skull and some smaller bones. The jute had been tied around the bag in a miniature replica of the ropes found on the victims Rainey believed were linked to Joshua Lee Hale's son. The jute ran through a hole punched in a manila shipping tag.

Wood picked up the clear evidence bag containing the tag and said, "It was rather thoughtful of the suspect to identify the victim." He handed the bag to Rainey. "The information does match an open missing person case. We're waiting for DNA confirmation."

Through the plastic, she read the neatly typed information on the tag, "Eileen Baker—Shipped January 29, 1999, from Portland, Maine." There were no other markings on the cardstock.

Dr. Munzer pointed at the tag. "Again, no prints. The lettering was done on a manual typewriter—old, maybe antique. Find the machine, we can match the strikers to the imprints on the paper."

Rainey returned the evidence bag to the table. She was drawn again to the jute. "This elaborate presentation and this specific knot, they serve no purpose other than to fulfill some element of the fantasy. These actions are compulsory to the unknown subject's crimes. It's part of his signature."

"Crimes? You are assuming this isn't a one-off," the doctor said.

"I've seen this knot before." Rainey turned to Wood. "What do we know about Eileen Baker?"

"She was a shift worker at Industrial Manufacturing by day and a local barfly by night. Hung out with the harbor crowd, commercial fishermen and charter fishing crews."

"How old?"

"Miss Baker was twenty-eight when she disappeared. She left her favorite bar at closing time and was never seen again."

Rainey thought aloud, "Well, that doesn't fit."

"Don't try to make it fit a theory or previous crime," Wood said. "Just look at what's here. What is this evidence telling you?"

Rainey took the prompt and began with the box.

"The box is ordinary, but the care to keep it clean of identifiers is extraordinary. I'm guessing the vacuum-sealed bag was just as clean?"

Dr. Munzer answered, "Yes. The skull and other bones in the bag were devoid of expected contaminants. My colleagues and I think it was processed and packaged in some sort of clean-room."

Rainey moved with SSA Wood to the table where the skull and its dislocated bottom jaw were displayed, as Dr. Munzer continued, "The remains were boiled, cleaned of tissue, soaked in bleach, and dried under a heat lamp or direct sunlight."

Rainey pointed at the horizontal divot and the hole it created in the skull. "This was the cause of death, I assume."

"The instrument she was struck with was slender, very hard, and attached to some kind of heavy dowel. It was strong enough to enter the skull. It would have been a death blow."

Rainey pointed at parallel scrapes on the surface of the skull. "These marks, I've seen this before when a body was left to forest scavengers. Do you think that's what happened here?"

"Well, yes, but not quite," Dr. Munzer said. She lifted the skull from the table. "We could identify deep scars in the bone from substantially large teeth. The measurement of the bite width indicates something sizeable. On the east coast, that's going to be a bear probably. I've called some fish and wildlife guys to take a look. Also, look here."

Munzer showed the base of the skull to the agents.

"See these striations. Under magnification, we were able to determine the skull was separated from the body with a saw. The tool marks indicate it was an industrial size bandsaw. The cervical bones that were cut are missing, but the saw struck the external occipital protuberance and shaved a sliver from the mastoid process over here. And to add to the mystery, the body was frozen before the skull was removed. The same holds true for the other bones here. The teeth marks overlay the saw marks."

Rainey nodded with understanding. "The body was frozen, cut into pieces, fed to an animal, recollected, processed in a clean room, and then delivered to the cops in an untraceable package. That's a lot of alone time with the body. This UNSUB has a private space to work."

Wood crossed his arms over his chest and took a step back from the evidence display. "Okay, Bell, what do you make of all this?"

"Because I'm here, which I don't believe is a coincidence, the freezing of the body, the head injury, and the knot could be associated with the four linked murders we discussed in my initial interview," Rainey answered. "But the age and area where she was taken do not match, so this could be a lesson in looking for clues to fit theories instead of theories that fit clues."

Wood remained quiet, while Rainey paused and thought carefully about what she would say next.

"Sir, if I was asked to analyze this murderer and it is murder just based on the tool marks—accident victims don't generally end up with their heads sawn off—I couldn't do it with just this evidence here. I could, but it would be incomplete and likely erroneous in many aspects."

Wood asked, "What isn't here? What can't you see?"

So this was a test. Rainey answered with confidence.

"Well, sir, I don't know who Eileen Baker was. I know her name, but I don't know how many drinks she had at her favorite bar, nor who she had them with. I don't know who saw her last and what they saw. What was the weather like? Was the moon out or was it a black night? Was there any evidence left behind? If not, is the lack of evidence significant?

"I don't know what Eileen's friends and family said about her. Was she good at her job? Was her barfly status a problem? Will anyone miss her? Would she give a stranger a ride? Did she have a routine? Did she drive or walk? Did she often engage in risky behavior, or was she streetwise and capable of taking care of herself?

"I need to study the victim to understand how she became one. I need the missing person report. I want to know who filed it. I need to see police reports, investigation notes, anything in the case file that can identify singular elements of this particular crime. I have to have comprehensive knowledge of the victim before I can understand the type of UNSUB that would murder her."

Wood nodded his agreement, but asked, "What can you tell me about the murderer, from just what you see?"

"He's organized, smart, meticulous, detail oriented. He plans things out and takes extreme precaution to leave no evidence behind. He most likely watched her for a few days before taking her. People probably saw him, but he blends into the crowd. He's nothing special. People that have met him can't really tell you anything about him. He's Mr. Nobody."

Rainey looked at the photos again, while she continued her evaluation of the evidence.

"He chose when and if the body would be discovered. The victim was taken in Maine, and the bones delivered to Florida almost a year to the date of her abduction. He has transportation and a private space to keep a live victim until she becomes a frozen one. We know he has a freezer large enough to hold a body and a bandsaw able to cut one up. He's confidently mobile. I'd say he is also single or has a job that leaves him free to move about untethered."

"Like a long-haul trucker?" Wood asked the question, verifying what Rainey was thinking.

"Yes, sir. Like a long-haul trucker with a freezer rig."

"Anything else?" Wood prodded. "How about age?"

"That's the most difficult element to predict. Given this level of preparation, patience, and follow-through, I think he's in his mid-thirties to mid-forties. If he's found to be younger, I wouldn't be surprised if he started killing in his teens."

Wood turned to Dr. Munzer. "You can show her."

Munzer's hand dropped into her lab coat pocket. She pulled out a small plastic see-through evidence bag.

"Don't break the seal," she said, before handing it to Wood.

He, in turn, handed the bag to Rainey.

"This was found in the bottom of the box. Do you recognize this card?"

Rainey saw right away that it was a standard bureau business card emblazoned with the Justice Department seal. She blinked once, then again to assure she read the name correctly. The card was hers. Rainey turned the card over and saw her handwriting on the back. She knew to whom she had given that particular card.

She met Wood's stare with, "Yes, sir. I know where this UNSUB has been, at least once."

"And where would that be?"

"He's been in my father's bail bonds business; specifically in my dad's office, where this card was removed from his desk."

"You're sure about that. You must hand out cards to lots of people. How do you know this one came from your father's office?"

"Because I wrote this address on the back when I moved to North Dakota. I saw it on his desk on at least three occasions since I gave it to him. It's the field office in Grand Rapids, where he sent my mail until I had my own address."

"We'll need to talk to him," Wood said, and then turned to say, "Thank you, Dr. Munzer."

He motioned for Rainey to return the evidence bag holding the card.

Rainey placed the card in Dr. Munzer's hand, said, "Thank you," and then scrambled to catch up with Wood who was already moving toward the door.

When she caught up, Wood said, "You know, Bell, everything isn't a test. You're in the BAU. You'll start in crimes against adults. That's what you wanted, isn't it?"

Rainey fought the urge to celebrate. "Yes, sir. Thank you for the vote of confidence, sir."

"You earned the position. Now go to work."

Boxing her soaring emotions for the moment, demonstrating the compartmentalization skills she had developed with the training to do the job, Rainey calmly commented on the case.

"Well, we know the UNSUB has an arrest history and where to look to find it. The only reason anyone would be in my dad's office would be to deal with a bail issue. This person was either arrested or signed for someone else that was."

"Is Chance Hale still in North Carolina?" Wood's mind had already gone where Rainey was trying to lead him.

"I don't know, sir, but I'm going to find out."

"Bell, are you concerned about your father. We can have a car sit on him till we catch this guy."

A little smile crept across Rainey's lips, not unnoticed by Wood.

"What are you finding amusing, Bell?"

"Oh, I wouldn't worry about Billy Bell, sir. He's more prepared than your average citizen for confrontations with a criminal like this one. Unless, of course, I'm entirely wrong about the UNSUB, and she's a good-looking woman with issues. Then he'll need help. He can't seem to see beyond the boobs to the agenda."

"Most of us can't," the twice-divorced Wood said with a chuckle.

#

"Billy Bell's Bail and Bait. This is Ernie speaking. How can I help you?"

No matter how many times Rainey heard Ernie answer the phone, it made her smile. Her dad's office manager had been a fixture in Rainey's life since she was ten-years-old. All was right with the world, as long as Ernie answered the phones at Billy Bell's Bail and Bait on Jordan Lake, in Chatham County, North Carolina.

"Hey, Ernie. It's Rainey."

"Well, good morning Agent Bell. "

"Good morning to you, too. Is Dad around?"

"No, honey. He's out with Mackie, picking up a skip."

"Well, you can probably help me more than he can."

"I can certainly try," Ernie said.

"Did you guys write paper on a Chance Obadiah Hale while I was in North Dakota. It would have been in 1998?"

"Let me look."

Rainey heard Ernie typing on the keyboard.

"No, I'm not seeing a Chance Hale."

"How about anyone with the last name Hale or associated with Hale Trucking?"

More keyboard typing produced an, "Aha! We have a Robby Hughes. His bail was set up and paid for by Obadiah Hale of Hale Trucking."

"Do you remember if either of them came to the office?"

"Well, it isn't the client I recall. It was the redhead your dad nearly married when she came through the door. She was absolutely his type, all made up and dressed to the nines."

"Oh, you know he secretly wishes you'd leave Henry and the boys and run off with him."

Ernie laughed. "If I run off, it won't be with Billy Bell, but Sean Connery. That I would do."

"Now I know why you made me watch all those James Bond movies with you and only the Connery ones."

"He's the real James Bond. The rest just wish they were him."

Rainey chuckled. "Does Henry know about this?"

"Honey, he does the best Sean Connery imitation. I just close my eyes and—"

38

"Hey, hey, hey. I don't need that much information about you and Henry Bond."

"We're consenting adults, Rainey. Grow up."

"I will never be grown enough to want to know about your fantasy life. Anyway, does that file give you the redhead's name?"

"Jean B. Berry, it says here. She came in to get the paperwork releasing the collateral used to secure the bail after, let me see, yes, the charges were dismissed."

"What were the charges?"

"Possession of a controlled substance, distribution to a minor, resisting arrest, assault on a police officer. It says Ketamine on the drug charge, so he probably lost his mind and raised some hell."

"When was that?"

"October of '98."

"Okay. That's what I needed. Thank you."

"Anytime," Ernie said, and then added in her version of a Connery accent, "Glad to be of service."

Rainey ended the call with a Bond impression too.

"Well done, Moneypenny."

7

June 29, 2005
Federal Bureau of Investigation
National Center for the Analysis of Violent Crime
Quantico, Virginia

"Special Agent Bell," Rainey said into the phone receiver, as she opened another file folder full of crime scene photos from Phoenix, where apparently two competing serial murderers were shooting people at random.

"Is this Rainey Bell, Billy Bell's kid?"

Rainey heard her father's name and came to attention.

"May I ask who's calling," she said, cautiously.

"Oh, I'm sorry. Sure, you wouldn't just tell that info to just anyone."

Rainey recognized the Dare County, North Carolina brogue, as the caller identified himself.

"This is Howard Daniel from Wanchese. Your daddy give me some money and your card in exchange for my promise to call you if I ever seen Chance Hale 'round here ag'in. I'm a man o' my word, so I'm a callin'."

"I appreciate your call, Mr. Daniel. So, Chance Hale is in Wanchese again?"

"Call me Howard. My daddy's Mr. Daniel. Yeah, ol' Chance rolled in a couple o' days ago. Took me a while to find what I done with your card, but I found it."

"I'm glad you did. If you keep this conversation quiet, I'll make sure my dad rewards you when he sees you again."

"I don't want to appear greedy, but when might that be, do you think?"

"He's heading down there this weekend for a two-week fishing binge."

"Well, I look forward to seeing him. Your daddy's good people."

"Yes, he is. Thanks again, Howard. You've been a big help."

Rainey hung up the phone and wrote the date on a sliver of paper. Using a pushpin, she attached the date to a wall-map of the US on the dot indicating Wanchese, a little fishing village in Dare County.

Chance Hale made his living as a commercial fishing industry mechanic and crewman. Rainey spent her own money and part of her precious little downtime tracking him and sending missing person flyers to his known locations. She went personally or sent her father to build a network of informants within the fishing community along the Atlantic coast. Chance, through his connection to the disappearance of Alyson Grayson, was Rainey's number one obsession. The inability to fulfill her promise to Alyson's mother was the albatross around her neck.

She kept a journal of Chance Hale's activities and the missing women cases that seemed to follow him from port to port. She sat back down at her desk, pulled the journal from her satchel, and opened it to the notation she made just two days ago. On Monday, Rainey recorded that Chance had been picked up and questioned in a sexual assault case. The victim was alive, but just barely. With no evidence to hold him on, the Newport News, Virginia police let him go when his lawyer showed up, but not before collecting DNA. Yesterday, Tuesday, another box of bones arrived at the FBI lab with "Attention: Special Agent R. B. Bell," written on the label. Again the remains were tagged, identifying the victim, the date, and the place of "shipment." The remains of Margaret Mary Hedrick of Newburyport, Massachusetts, became the sixth box of bones received since January of 2000. The bones had been left in a lifeguard stand in Virginia Beach.

"Bell."

SSA Wood's voice interrupted Rainey, just as she was about to note Chance's current whereabouts for her records. She looked up to see Wood standing just outside her cubicle.

Rainey acknowledged his presence with, "SSA Wood, sir." She began to stand out of respect.

"No, no, don't get up. I hear another box of bones came in."

"Yes, sir."

"Same story, no trace evidence?"

"Yes, sir."

"Still think that Hale boy from Carolina is involved?"

41

"It's the same UNSUB sending the boxes. I know that. And I'm sure we'll be able to tie Chance Hale to this victim too, but again, it'll all be circumstantial. He's involved. Either he is the UNSUB, or the UNSUB wants us to believe he is. There is no such thing as that many circumstantial meetings with women who end up as murder victims."

Wood eyed the map on the wall. "Where is he now?"

"He left Newport News after being questioned in a sexual assault last weekend. The victim lived, but with head trauma too severe to remember anything right now. She might recover some memories, but they'd be unreliable after she's been repeatedly told what happened to her. Chance is in Wanchese currently. He's circling closer to home these days."

Wood stared at the map for a bit and then turned his focus on Rainey. "Look, oversight says you haven't taken even one of the mandatory mental health days this year. I am told you have ten days of leave. Make arrangements and let me know when you'll be gone."

It sounded like a polite request, but it wasn't. It was an order given in Wood's subtle management style.

"Yes, sir," Rainey answered.

"Good then," Wood said before starting away.

Rainey stopped him with, "Sir?"

Wood turned back to face her. "Yes, Bell."

"May I take ten days starting Friday? My father has a cottage in Nags Head for two weeks. I think the salt air would do me good."

Wood's lips curled into a perceptive smile. "Sounds great. Enjoy the sun. Give your father my regards."

"I will, sir. Thank you, sir."

8

January 10, 2009
Volusia County Jail
Red John Drive
Daytona Beach, Florida

"Chance Obadiah Hale. We meet again."

"Very Special Agent Rainey Blue Bell. I've always thought your name was like a weather report and a country song scrambled together."

Eleven years had passed since their first meeting on a frigid morning in North Dakota. It had been four years since she had seen him across a gravel parking lot, headed for a trawler with a duffel bag slung over his shoulder. Chance had celebrated his twenty-seventh birthday four days before this meeting. It was also the day of his arrest for killing a woman.

He had sutures above his right eye and a purple bruise on the corresponding jawline. Still scrawny with the same stringy, sun-bleached blond hair, maintained the surfer boy wiriness and emotive sadness the teen girls had found alluring, except it had morphed into more of an unattractive drunken beach bum vibe. The dark bruise on his jaw made the thin patches of facial hair on his chin more noticeable. It was the type of scraggly beard grown by young fair-haired men who really shouldn't bother. Rainey thought either the glare of the fluorescent lights bounced off Chance's jail-orange jumpsuit and caused the jaundiced tint to his angler's tan, or the kidneys and liver of the young but dedicated alcoholic had begun to fail.

She responded to his critique of her name. "I have to admit, Chance O. Hale has given me a chuckle or two. Our parents had imagination, if not forethought."

"I had fucked up parents. I bet yours weren't much better."

Rainey smiled and observed her obsession up close for the first time since they occupied that kitchen table in Joshua Lee Hale's home; back when "that Hale boy from Carolina" was an arrogant teenager full of hidden patricidal rage. Rainey had discovered, in the years since that explosive first meeting, Chance Hale had a good reason for his detached reaction to his father's death.

She kept smiling during her response. "My parents? No, they were just two normal high school seniors with raging hormones."

"Backseat baby," was Chance's low energy comment. He'd spent his momentary spike in adrenaline on his original dig.

He was, as they say in recovery circles, unwell. His skin glistened with sweat. Strands of unruly hair clung to his clammy forehead. His voice quivered, and his body shook with each wave of bone-chilling nausea. He had been under medically observed acute alcohol withdrawal for the last seventy-two hours. The bucket on the floor next to his chair indicated he had not cleared the puking stage.

Rainey opened the folder in front of her, pretending to review the material she knew without the refresher, while nonchalantly replying to his comment.

"My parents eloped after graduation and ran away to the Outer Banks to become hippies. My name seems fitting for that narrative." She paused to raise her green eyes to meet Chance's faded blue ones. "However, I do agree with you on your parentage. 'Fucked up' doesn't really begin to describe the depravity surrounding your conception."

Chance wiped the sweat-drenched hair from his forehead with his right hand. His handcuffed left hand followed with no alternative. The movement caused the correctional officer in the corner to take a step forward. Chance glanced over his shoulder, eyeing his captor with a glint of fear before quickly dropping his hands to the tabletop. The CO relaxed, and Chance returned his attention to Rainey.

"I figured when I gave that DNA in Virginia you'd get wind of it and it wouldn't be long before you put a few things together. Care to share the revolting details?"

Rainey knew Chance wanted to know if what he suspected about his heritage was true. She needed him bruised and tender. It was a win for both of them. He was weak from the forced sobriety. The truth might soften him further. Rainey wanted a confession. She wanted to know who killed the six women in the boxes that had come once a year from 2000 through 2005. She wanted to know what happened to Alyson Grayson.

She revealed her knowledge of his genealogy with the sole purpose of abating his defenses.

"We tested DNA found in the explosion that killed most of your family. We ran it against yours. Joshua Lee Hale, the man you believed to be your father, was really your half-brother. His father, Obadiah Hale, is also your biological father. Your aunt Sarah was your half-sister."

Rainey watched his reaction. Chance paid close attention to what she said and appeared unsurprised. She went for the worst of it.

"But that isn't the whole story, is it? Instead of running off with another man, as you were told, your mother probably died trying to get away from the hell she left you in—but then again, her body was never found. If she's still alive somewhere, that would mean she got away but didn't care enough to come back for you after your father blew himself up, and not even after everyone else died in the explosion that leveled old man Hale's house. The house you were supposed to be sleeping in, by the way. Have you ever wondered why?"

Chance shrugged indifference, but Rainey knew he had wondered. It ate at him, according to the journals they found in his truck.

She continued, "The lab noticed something about your DNA. Let me see. I have a report here that explains the findings in layman's terms. It can be confusing."

She flipped through some pages in the file, stopping on the one she wanted, before beginning to read.

"Your DNA shows an 'absence of heterozygosity.' See, it says that right here." She slid the paper in front of Chance and pointed at the pertinent sentence, as she explained, "This means that large chunks of your mother and father's contributions to your DNA are identical because they shared much of their genetic code. In other words, it is very likely that they were first-degree relatives, as in father and daughter or brother and sister. I think you see what this means."

She waited for Chance's eyes to leave the paper and re-establish eye contact with her, before asking. "Are those the few things we may have learned that you were referring to?"

"I suppose that's enough."

"Well, no, not really, Chance. Let's talk about why I'm here and the stuff in the toolbox on the back of your truck. That's a little fucked up too, don't you think?"

"Well, yeah, if you don't know what it is."

"I'm going to let you tell me what it is, but first I need to know you have been read your rights and are speaking to me at your request without a lawyer."

"Yeah, I told 'em to call you."

Rainey pointed at the one-way glass. "You acknowledge there is a camera aimed at us and that you are being recorded. Is that correct?"

Chance nodded.

"I need you to answer verbally, for the record."

"Yes, I am talking to you without a lawyer on the record. Okay? Can we get on with it?"

"Are you under arrest, Chance?"

"Yes, but you know that."

"I need anyone who reviews this interview to know. I want no part of an illegal interview that might someday set you free. Why are you in jail in Daytona Beach, Florida?

Chance dropped his chin to his chest before answering, "I'm under arrest for vehicular homicide. I fell asleep at the wheel and drove my truck into oncoming traffic. I hit a car head-on."

Rainey filled in the details Chance shied away from. "You killed a young mother and put both of her children in intensive care. Your blood alcohol concentration was point-two-nine. Is that correct?"

Chance kept his chin tucked and his eyes focused on the tabletop, when he answered softly, "Yes."

"So, you realize you are going to prison and talking with me will have no bearing on the vehicular homicide charge. Is that correct?"

"Yes," Chance said, this time raising his head to face Rainey.

"All right, then," Rainey said and then asked, "Why did you call for me, Chance? What is it that you think I can do for you?"

"Maybe you can explain to these yahoos down here that I'm being set up with that serial killer shit."

"What makes you think I can do that, Chance? I've looked over this evidence. It's pretty compelling."

"I did not kill those women. Someone put that stuff in my toolbox. Joshua Hale was a killer, not me."

"Your fingerprints are all over the toolbox, inside and out. You also handled every piece of evidence found inside. If it isn't yours, how did that happen?"

"It's my fucking toolbox. It'd be damn strange if my prints weren't on it. And I touched all those bags of stuff when I found it, but I didn't open them."

"What do you mean by 'found it'?"

"When I came back to the states, I didn't expect my shit to still be where I left it. I mean, I got on the boat that mornin' and I didn't plan to come back."

Rainey looked down and pretended to read her notes.

46

"In your statement to the investigators, you say you came back to the US because the Brazilian authorities suspected you in a series of missing women cases. Is that correct?"

"Behind bars in Brazil is no place to be, man. Hell yeah, I left. They're just looking for a scapegoat. Somebody told 'em I was there, that my dad was a serial killer, and that I was wanted for a bunch of murders in the states. Who the fuck does that? Find out who is stalking me, telling lies about me, and you'll know who put that stuff in my truck."

Rainey made a note just so he'd see she was listening to him. She gave the impression that his story had value, but she could not let him control how he told it.

"Hang on. Let's back up a sec," Rainey said, leaning a little closer, giving Chance full eye contact—hoping he would see genuine interest in his story. She loved this part of her job. During the last nine years in the Behavioral Analysis Unit, Rainey had come to enjoy the conversations with criminals, especially those who underestimated her knowledge of their crimes. Moving Chance through his timeline without continuity kept him off balance.

"You say you took a trawler out of Wanchese to South America in July 2005. Is that right?"

"Yeah. I had to go, man. Somebody was stalking me. Stuff was happening all the time. I just knew whoever it was couldn't follow me out to sea. I took the mechanic job on the trawler *Apple's Eye* for a ride down to Brazil. Worked out of Santos, São Paulo, till the police started dogging me."

Rainey knew all about the stalker. In July of 2005, she took ten days off work to vacation with her father in Nags Head, just a few miles from the Wanchese docks. Chance had recently arrived from Newport News, Virginia. He had been questioned, gave a voluntary DNA sample, and was released in the abduction of Donna Hollis Travis. Rainey's presence was not a coincidence. Chance indeed had a stalker at the time, an FBI agent who didn't want him to get too comfortable.

Despite being a barely functioning drunk, Chance was a hell of a mechanic. He traveled up and down the east coast, from dock to dock. Truly gifted with engines of all types, he picked up odd jobs and on rare occasions signed on for a steady paycheck with a captain willing to overlook his alcohol addiction. Amazingly, Chance had become proficient at maintenance drinking when out at sea, nipping just enough to keep the tremors at bay.

When he was on shore, he stayed at the docks in his truck. Chance Hale lived a simple life, despite being heir to half of Hale Trucking. He'd been to Wanchese before and had crewed with some of the captains, so the locals welcomed him back. It cost Rainey a leap of faith and a hundred bucks upfront, but it paid off when her phone rang the minute Chance Hale had returned to Dare County.

Rainey arrived a week after Chance, and with her came the flyers for missing women connected to the fishing industry. Flyers started showing up on the windshields of vehicles parked at the docks and the bulletin boards at local fisherman hangouts. While the flyers did not name Chance as a suspect, they certainly played a part in his leaving when he did. Rainey had no idea it would be four years before he returned. At least the boxes of bones with her name on them stopped arriving once a year after he sailed away. But Chance didn't know of her involvement in his misery beyond her official capacity as a federal agent.

She asked, "Somebody was stalking you? Can you tell me more about that?"

"I guess you know about the girl in Newport News."

She did, but asked, "What girl?"

"Okay, back in 2005, this girl I had a few drinks with—Donna, her name was Donna—well, she ended up gettin' attacked. They asked me questions. I gave them answers. They let me go. Just like always."

"Were you a suspect?"

"I'm always a suspect. I've been a suspect since Alyson disappeared, but you know that. "

"You've left a lot of unanswered questions and missing women in your wake, Chance. I think that's why you are, as you say, 'always a suspect.' I doubt my inquiries into your whereabouts and activities have caused you the trouble those missing women have."

"People go missing all the time. Why am I always a suspect?"

"Since 1998, seven women known to you have disappeared. The partial remains of six of them have been recovered. An eighth, Donna Travis, was abducted and raped. She escaped with permanent brain trauma. Her attacker did not intend for her to live. That many women who know you have been murdered or almost killed. That's just not the average person's reality, Chance."

"That's what I've been trying to tell you. It ain't normal."

The correctional officer tried unsuccessfully to stifle a snort. Rainey cut her eyes in his direction, before redirecting Chance.

"So, this 'girl you had a few drinks with' is assaulted, you're questioned, and then let go. How does that tie in with the toolbox full of evidence indicating you may be a serial rapist and murderer?"

Chance sighed, defeated. "I don't know why I even try. You've been tryin' to lock me up since I was sixteen for a murder I didn't commit."

"Murder? Is Alyson dead, Chance?"

"She's been gone for eleven years. If she was alive, I imagine we'd know about it by now, don't you?"

"Until I find out what happened to Alyson after she left the lake with you, I'll keep asking the question. Where is Alyson, Chance?"

"I don't want to talk about Alyson. I asked for you so you can explain to these people that I am not a serial murderer. You do this for a living now, right? Profile me. I'm a drunk, but I'm not a killer."

One corner of Rainey's mouth rose slowly in a half-smiling smirk. "You're a drunk and a killer, Chance. We established that at the beginning of this interview." Before he could react, she changed directions again. "Now, tell me about the stuff in the toolbox. If you didn't put it there, how did it get there?"

Agitated, Chance snapped back, "For all I know, you put it there."

Rainey was quick with her emotionless answer, "Nope. Try again."

A flustered Chance rapidly spit out his story before Rainey could interrupt him again. "I left my truck in Wanchese at my friend Howard Daniel's house."

Rainey couldn't help but think Chance had no idea his friend Howard was a rat, but she said nothing as he continued to explain.

"I came back to the states on a trawler that was headed home to Wanchese. When I got back, Howard says my truck is where I left it. I found them newspaper articles, pictures, and stuff in the toolbox, all sealed in plastic, and clean, as if it hadn't been there long. I'm thinking, how did anyone know I was back in the states before I got here? I got my truck runnin', threw some new tires on her, and got the hell out of there."

"Why didn't you leave the toolbox? Why not throw it away?"

Chance leaned toward Rainey to support his sincerity. "I thought it would be good evidence that I am being set up."

Rainey couldn't hide her amusement this time. "So you drove to Florida with a toolbox full of evidence that implicates you in several murders as proof you aren't a murderer. That is certainly an interesting strategy."

Everyone in the room heard the loud, gravelly voice coming down the hallway. It wasn't a voice raised in anger. It sounded like a man engaged in a backslapping laugh with an old friend. The bolt on the door clanged open. The two men still chuckled as they entered.

The big-voiced older gentleman held an unlit cigar stub in the corner of his cheek-consuming smile. He gave the man with him a last pat on the shoulder, as he said, "You come on up to Tybee and we'll drink Scotch, go fishing, and let the widows from the condos fawn over us."

The balding crown of the shoulder pat recipient's head blushed red, which was made more pronounced by the white hair that surrounded it. He smiled at his friend, drawling shyly, "I doubt there would be much fawning over an old, balding, out of shape man like me."

Cigar man said, "If your heart's beating and your pecker works, they'll be interested." He followed this pronouncement with a deep chested chuckle that vibrated the room.

The jovial tone changed rather rapidly, as Rainey was let in on the identities of the two men. Cigar man went first.

"You must be Special Agent Rainey Bell," he said, sticking out a meaty hand for a shake. "My name is Horace Blackman. I know your daddy. Fine fellow, just fine. I represent Mr. Hale and am bringing this interview to a halt."

Rainey rose to her feet and shook his hand. "Mr. Blackman. I was under the impression you had retired to Georgia."

"I have and you are well-informed, but there's a redhead in Carolina that has my number, so to speak." He turned his attention to Chance. "You look like hell, young man. You'll feel better when you dry out. I'll see to it that you continue to receive excellent medical care for the duration of your rehabilitation."

"Thank you, Mr. Blackman," Chance said politely.

"Now," Horace said, focusing on Rainey again, "I thought you knew better than to speak with a lawyered up suspect."

"Your client waved his right to counsel and consented to speak with me on the record. Mr. Blackman, Chance called me."

The balding man introduced himself next.

"Ms. Bell, my name is Richard George. I'm with the State Attorney's office. Information has come to light that precludes your further involvement in any investigations concerning Mr. Hale. Your superiors have been informed."

Rainey bristled at the dismissal of her official status. "It's Special Agent Bell, Mr. George." Rainey was used to power plays within the justice system. She also suspected a little collusion between these two old friends. "What information?"

George's smug look signaled Rainey wasn't going to like what he was about to say.

"We have the results from the fingerprint and DNA analysis on the articles inside the vacuum-sealed bags found in the toolbox. Maybe you would like to explain how your prints were found on several of the flyers and the Virginian-Pilot article about Donna Travis's assault."

Rainey had a suspicion as to how her prints ended up in the toolbox collection of murder memorabilia found on Chance Hale. If he knew she was posting the flyers, he could have grabbed a few. Maybe he saw her reading the paper in the parking lot. Maybe she wasn't as good at surveillance as she thought. Either way, this conversation was out of line.

"Isn't it highly improper to have this discussion in front of the defense, sir?"

Blackman chuckled again. "Just like your daddy. Full of spit and vinegar, smart too."

Rainey turned to the attorney. "I'm sorry, what?"

"Your daddy and I go back to my Durham attorney days. I just now spoke with him. I gave him a call when his fingerprints also turned up on some of the evidence. While I don't believe you or Billy Bell did anything improper, I assure you I can convince a jury that you did. I convinced ol' Dick here in about five minutes."

Rainey's mouth fell open.

Blackman turned to Chance. "Son, you're going to prison. I cut you a deal for fifteen years on a vehicular manslaughter charge. Take it. You'll be out in eight to ten."

"Fifteen years," Chance repeated, as if saying it made it real.

"That's a hell of a deal, son. Florida doesn't take too kindly to drunks taking mommas from babies while on family vacation. It isn't good for business. With your record of DUIs and other marks on your past, Mr. George here could make a case for throwing away the key. Of course, I wouldn't let him, but in the meantime, I'd have the rest of that inheritance as my down payment."

Chance asked, "What about the toolbox, the missing women?"

Mr. George closed the matter.

"Mr. Hale, the evidence is compromised. The State Attorney's office has no further questions at this time." He turned to Rainey. "Special Agent Bell, I believe you're wanted back at Quantico. Good evening."

And with that, the albatross would be left to rot in one of the boxes in Rainey's compartmentalized world of emotions. She went back to Quantico. The fact that her fingerprints were on flyers she put up was no surprise to anyone. Chance went to prison. No more skulls or bones arrived in boxes with Rainey's name on them. Alyson Grayson's mother still prayed every night to find her girl. Years rolled by and the investigation into Chance Hale's involvement in the disappearance of seven women went deeply cold, until...

PART II

"Since then, at an uncertain hour,
That agony returns:
And till my ghastly tale is told,
This heart within me burns."
— Samuel Taylor Coleridge,
The Rime of the Ancient Mariner

9

August 29, 2016
Bulls Bay, Albemarle Sound
Northeast coast of North Carolina

"It's getting choppy up here. If you don't find it in the next two minutes, I'm calling it. It's lightning on the south side of Roanoke Island."

The hollow-sounding voice of the diver returned through the speaker, "Give me five, Carter. I know it's here."

"The fall semester started today, and this equipment was due back to the department last Friday. This cloud is an omen, Rye. Time to call it a summer."

"Hold on, I see something."

Carter rolled his eyes at his research partner, though she could not see him. Rye was somewhere beneath the boat searching the Albemarle Sound bottom for wreckage of ancient sea craft.

Replying to Rye's "hold on" request, Carter said into the headset microphone, "Those words I want on a tee shirt. The mantra of the summer of 2016."

"No, really. Under all this vegetation, there's a...I don't know. It's definitely the source of the rectangular object on the sonar...but I don't think..."

The sounds of grunting filled Carter's headset. "Hey, Rye. Are you all right?"

"Yeah, I'm just trying to move some more of this vegetation." Another grunt preceded the rest of the communication. "Crap, it's just a couple of crab pots that got tangled together. They look weird though—"

"Okay, come on up," Carter said, already standing and looking southward to the darkening sky. "Don't rush. But we really need to get going."

Over two hundred vessels had gone down in the shallow Albemarle Sound. He did not want to add to that number. Shallow sounds could make for violent water in the right circumstances. It was ninety degrees in the sun a few minutes ago. The temperature was dropping as the coming squall drew the breeze off the water. Standing in the shallow-drafting small whaler, Carter was listening for the thunder after the most recent flash of lightning in the distant clouds.

"Oh my, god! Oh my, God!" Rye's voice exploded in his ears.

"What!" Carter jumped, jolted from cloud-watching by the panicked voice from below. Then remembering his job to keep his diver safe, he spoke with calm authority into the microphone, "Do not freak out. You're underwater, albeit shallow, you need the full minute to surface unless this is an emergency worth a bad decompression experience."

"Carter! There's a skull in there."

"Shit, Rye. Did we actually find the wreck?"

"No, in the crab pot, or whatever it is. There's...oh my, god!"

"Stop saying that."

"Carter, I'm coming up, and you need to make two phone calls. One to tell Dr. Heidnik that his equipment will be later than expected and so will we."

"Why? What is it, Rye? What did you find?"

Rye ignored his questions and continued, "The second call"—a chuckle interrupted her, more as a nervous release than humor—"well, I guess that really should be your first. Call 9-1-1. You're reporting the remains of a murder victim."

"How do you know it's a murder victim?"

Carter heard only breathing in return.

He repeated, "How do you know it was murder? I can't just call and say we found a murder victim in a crab pot. Why can't I just say 'remains' and let them figure out what happened? It could just be a fisherman that fell in by accident."

His diver broke the surface behind the boat. Carter reached out and took the fins held up to him and then helped Rye navigate the ladder. Once onboard, the heavy sigh from the other side of the mask encouraged Carter to hurry his assistance with its removal, as Rye flopped onto the seat.

Once free of the mask and after a few deep, slow breaths, Rye pushed the neoprene cap from her head and rubbed her fingers through her sun-streaked hair. She had arrived with long monochrome brunette waves. The longest hair on her head was now three inches. It had been a summer of changes. She looked up at her research partner. Carter stood with his phone in one hand and a bottle of water in the other.

"Carter, I can't imagine under what circumstances one would find an accidental or natural death victim inside a crab pot out in the middle of the sound. Can you?"

Carter handed her the water bottle and then immediately made the call.

"Yeah, hey, we're out in the Albemarle Sound, just off Bulls Bay, and well, we found a body. We think it's a murder victim."

Rye watched Carter nod to the voice on the other end of the call.

He turned to face her when he said into the receiver. "Well, it's a body stuffed inside a crab pot at the bottom of the sound. What would you think happened?"

He paused to listen, before reading off the coordinates from the onboard GPS. Rye looked over the side, remembering the remains of a life trapped there on the bottom.

She whispered over the waves chopping at the hull. "You're not alone anymore. They're coming. They're coming."

10

January 14, 2017
Former home of Joshua Lee Hale
Pembina, North Dakota

"I'm telling you, it's coming from this wall. Here, smell right here."

"Oh, I believe you, Mr. Kirby. I can smell it from where I'm standing."

"Oh," Sydney Kirby said to the contractor. "I guess I've smelled it so long, I don't get the full effect until I get right up against this wall. Pretty rank, huh?"

"Yes, it is," Jim Jarrett said, as he moved over to the wall and began running his hand along the surface. He looked up at the joint where the wall met the ceiling and then turned back to his client. "Mr. Kirby, do you know who used to live in this house."

Sydney nodded his head. "Yes, a serial killer lived here. I know the story."

Jim asked, "Do you know when this doorway was closed up and the wall resurfaced?"

"No. I wasn't aware of any old doorway. I had a water pipe leak right over there." He pointed about five feet from the resurfaced area. "We fixed that, but left the rest of the wall alone."

"Well, you can see the doorway, if you know what to look for, especially if the job wasn't that well done."

"Where would a door go? We're in the basement."

"Mr. Kirby, I think there is another room on the other side of this wall, and someone didn't want it found."

"Get the fuck outta here," Sydney said.

"I'll be happy to open it back up for you, but considering the smell, I'd suggest you go ahead and call the police. If it isn't a body, it's probably something else you and I do not want any part of."

"Maybe it's a sewage pipe or something."

Jim smiled. "Mr. Kirby, I've been doing this a long time. I know what shit smells like. That smell right there is rotting flesh."

"But that Hale guy blew himself up almost twenty years ago. How would there be a body just now smelling?"

"Global warming," Jim said. "Maybe she's just now thawing out."

"No, seriously. How could a body last that long underground?"

Jim picked up a giant sledgehammer. "Only one way to find out," he said, before taking a big swing at the wall.

The first hit sent drywall flying. Sydney took a step back. The second crushed the concrete block filler behind it. The third sent cold, putrid air surging into the room. Jim covered his nose and mouth with a rag he quickly drew from his pocket. Sydney turned green and tried not to gag as he pulled the cell phone from his pocket. Jim used his free hand to fish a small pin light from his pocket. He pointed it through the hole he had created into what appeared to be a tunnel. His light hit an old decaying freezer sitting in a puddle of goo.

Jim asked, "Did you cut any wires when you worked on the leak?"

From under the collar of his sweatshirt pulled up over his nose, Sydney replied. "Yes. They found a junction box and wire that looked like it ran out of the house underground, maybe to the old garage foundation behind the house. From what they told me, it was an add-on to the original wiring and a fire hazard hidden in the wall that way. They cut it, and nothing stopped working. So I assumed they were right."

"Well, something stopped working, Mr. Kirby and it's the source of your smell. There's a freezer behind this wall. Care to guess what's inside?" Jim looked back at his dazed customer, who stood still holding the phone, immobile. He asked through the cloth over his mouth, "Not sure who to call, huh?"

Sydney shook his head. "I figured I'd just call 9-1-1. I'm just trying to decide how to say I think a serial killer left a body at my house."

Jim chuckled through the cloth. "I think that'll probably get the kind of folks you're looking for on the move."

Sydney fought another gag reflex and said, "Yeah, that'll probably do it."

11

March 24, 2017
The Bell-Meyers Residence
Chatham County, NC

"Hey! No hitting," Mack exclaimed.

"That's a yellow card, Weather," Timothy, the rule follower explained.

"Weather, I think you need to take a timeout."

"But Nee Nee, Mack keeps catching the ball."

Rainey looked down at the little blonde storming her way, hands on hips. Except for the green eyes, she was a miniature of her mother. Not only did Weather look like Katie, she also matched her in fiery determination. She stomped toward Rainey with her jaw set hard and her brow knitted.

"He won't let me kick it in the net," she complained.

"Honey, he's playing goalie. You are supposed to try to kick it where he can't catch it. However, you are not supposed to hit him when he does."

"That's not fair," Weather said, adding a foot stomp for effect.

"Actually, it is fair. Those are the rules. If you want to play the game, play by the rules. Otherwise, you can play by yourself or help me by watering the garden."

Satisfied that her options were thoroughly explained, Weather transformed from disgruntled preschooler to perfect child in a flash. She stuck out her hand and smiled sweetly.

"Can I water the garden, please?"

"Yes, you may."

Despite the display of manners, Rainey held fast to the nozzle. "Water hose rules: no spraying me, or Danny, or your brothers, or the dog, or anyone. Just spray in the beds where we planted the vegetables Ernie and Henry gave us." It was best to be specific.

"Okay."

"Promise?"

An impatient sigh preceded Weather's, "I promise."

Rainey made sure the nozzle setting wouldn't allow Weather to destroy the tender seedlings and then handed the hose over with some trepidation.

Pointing at the raised beds, she said, "Go. Farm. Be one with nature."

Danny McNally chuckled as he followed Rainey through the backyard.

He commented, "The behavioral analyst in me finds these little developing personalities fascinating. The man in me finds that little girl's prospects almost chilling. She'll win her share of battles simply by willing it so."

Rainey smiled over her shoulder and said, "I'm married to her mother. It's a shared genetic trait."

In the outdoor kitchen, Rainey checked the beef ribs on the grill. They had been smoking since early morning. Turkey burgers for the kids waited in the fridge, having been cooked while the coals were glowing hot at sunrise. She made potato salad, coleslaw, and started the baked beans during naptime, finishing just before Danny and his girlfriend, Cathleen, arrived.

As Danny peered over her shoulder into the grill, he said in a horrible attempt at imitating Sir David Attenborough's naturalist narration, "Look closely at the thoroughly domesticated Rainey Blue Bell in her natural setting. She cooks, she wrangles kids, and she solves cold case crimes in her spare time."

"What spare time? I have a never-ending stack of cases to review. Sadly, the cold case business is booming. I took the day off because you were coming in and Katie had a full day of meetings after preschool this morning."

Danny and his girlfriend had flown down from DC earlier in the day. Danny had decided to extend a formal visit into a mini-vacation. An official request had come from the FBI, asking Rainey to interview a prisoner, Chance Hale. She agreed if only to facilitate the BAU getting a crack at the one she let get away. It had been nearly twenty years since Alyson Grayson went missing. The albatross still hung heavy on Rainey, after all these years.

Danny tossed his empty beer bottle in the trashcan and fetched another from the little refrigerator under the bar. "Do you need a cold one?"

Rainey shook her head. "No, I'm good. I have to sip until I'm off kid duty, then I'll throw a few back with you."

"I understand. If you don't mind, I'll get a head start. I'm trying to wash the DC bullshit out of my throat," Danny said. "Same reason Cathleen needed a shower. Washington leaves a stench these days." He stared across the yard into the waning sun and then changed the subject. "They sure are growing up fast. Five years seems like a minute ago."

Danny engaged in superficial conversation, but his deeper thoughts were elsewhere. Rainey could wait him out. He'd talk when he was ready.

He covered his dark mood with a chuckle and asked, "Which was harder, working at the Bureau or raising kids?"

"The Bureau was less unpredictable than keeping up with three five-year-olds," Rainey said. "Having Weather in the mix adds a further degree of difficulty. She's definitely the ringleader when trouble is afoot. Though I observe her corruptive powers over her brothers with more curiosity than concern."

Danny grinned at Rainey. "Ah yes, a brilliant strategist or a criminal mastermind?"

"A bit of both, I'd say. I've found it best to be straightforward with Weather. The boys are easier, both motivated by praise and eager to please."

"I have observed the group dynamic of triplet-land from the beginning. Jolly, momma's boy Mack, taller and thicker than his brother, is the muscle. Lanky, serious Timothy is the thinker. Together, they form petite and charming Weather's minions." Danny nodded in the little girl's direction. "She isn't necessarily an obstinate child, but she is willing..."

Rainey finished the description for Weather's Godfather, "to push every boundary, ask unlimited questions, and apparently prefers debate to compliance until satisfied all alternatives have been exhausted."

Danny tipped the top of his beer toward Rainey. "I was going to say, like you, Weather sometimes weighs the punishment against the reward and goes for it."

"Let's hope her lessons are not as painful as mine."

Rainey did a surveillance sweep of the yard almost without thinking about it. The soccer ball lay forgotten in the back of the net. Fifteen feet away, Timothy and Mack were on their knees, heads pressed together and noses six inches from the grass. They were engrossed in the activities of a tiny living creature of some sort. Rainey hoped it would not end up in a pocket to be found later by an unsuspecting parent. It took a good full-body shudder to be rid of the memory of the warm, but very dead toad in the tiny pocket of Mack's recently vacated jeans.

Carl was nose down in the grass near the large cedar play set. At almost eighteen months old, he was being the part hound dog that he was, which involved sniffing out the cat's hiding place. Freddie, the cat, watched from his perch atop the slide. Theirs was a relationship still in development. Clearly, Freddie's advantage was age and wisdom, along with the fact he did not desire to be Carl's friend, now or ever.

All of her charges accounted for, Rainey took a quick glance to assure Weather still had the hose aimed at the plants.

"Hey, Weather. Move to the next bed, honey. I think that one is wet enough." Rainey gave Weather, who was soaking wet from her belly down, a thumbs-up and a big smile. "Good job."

Just behind her, verifying what Rainey already knew, Danny's warm baritone said sweetly, "You have a beautiful life."

Rainey turned back to face him, smiling widely. "I really do. I could not have dreamed this life. In fact, I'm quite sure it never crossed my mind until it happened."

Weather said, "I'm finished, Nee Nee," as she dropped the hose in front of Rainey. "Mommy's home."

The landing of the hose at her feet engaged the handle on the nozzle, which showered Rainey with a quick cold blast to the face.

Rainey gasped.

Weather giggled.

"Good one," Danny said when he high-fived Weather as she ran by.

After the initial shock, Rainey grabbed the nozzle and chased her delighted daughter a few steps. She stopped, adjusted the nozzle to jet spray, and then fired the hose at Weather's heels, just to hear her squeal and cackle with laughter as she ran toward her mother.

Katie had entered the scene with a cell phone pressed to her ear. Rainey shut off the hose, which stopped the squealing in time to hear Katie respond to the person on the phone with, "My religion?"

Politics, it would seem, had not yet lost its grasp today. Though the thought of a very public and politically engaged Katie Bell-Meyers sent Rainey's paranoia meter into the red, she was riveted to her wife's every word. Danny was too. Katie had a gift and a calling. People had suggested she use that gift and run for office.

A former Republican politician's wife—albeit a serial killer whom Katie swore would have been a rock star in the current administration if she hadn't blown a hole in his chest with a shotgun— Katie Bell-Meyers was now a poster child for activist, Democratic Party women; one with connections across the aisle. Katie knew where weaknesses lay and skeletons rattled, which enabled her to motivate a stubborn state legislator when she had to. It scared Rainey to death.

She and Danny could hear only Katie's side of the conversation.

"Hmmm—Do you mean a particular system of faith?"

Katie placed her oversized purse on the patio table, smiled and waved at Rainey and Danny with her free hand, and knelt to receive the triplets running her way, one of whom was more than slightly damp. She did all of this while giving the conversation its due attention.

"Ah, yes, I see. Well then, I suppose I do. My 'religion' is my faith in the basic goodness of man, my belief in the importance of overcoming ignorance, and the recognition of human rights for all regardless of race, religion, gender, or sexuality; the rights to life, liberty, and the pursuit of happiness among them."

The kids crashed into Katie, knocking her off kilter. The four of them became a ball of giggling triplets wrapped around their mother, rolling about in the grass.

She laughed into the phone and said, "And now I have to go spend the weekend with the family you want to vote out of existence. Do you hear that laughter? That's the generation that will make dinosaurs like you obsolete. Good night, Senator."

#

"That's not what happened," Rainey contended, as she leaned forward to stoke the outdoor fire pit.

"Then you tell it," Danny retorted.

Danny's girlfriend Cathleen Augustine laughed. "Somebody tell it. Don't leave me hanging."

"Katie was stressed out and scared. She had too much to drink, and Cookie should have—"

The back door opened, and Katie reappeared carrying the two-way baby monitor. The talkback button was a necessity in a three-story house. Mommy, as an ever-present voice, squashed rebellions before they made it down the stairs most nights.

She noticed the conversation stopped on her arrival and asked with a grin, "Were you talking about me?"

Without seeing the grimaces on Danny and Rainey's faces in the dim firelight, Cathleen answered, "They were telling me about the time you punched out a reporter."

"We've known you two years, and they're just getting around to sharing that? You two are slacking," Katie said to Danny and Rainey, followed by a genuine laugh.

63

This relieved Rainey, but she still defended herself. "Danny was telling it. I was correcting him."

"Right. Throw me under the bus," Danny said.

"You don't have to live with her," Rainey countered.

Katie sat down next to Rainey on one of the patio loveseats, as she commented, "I should think you'd be glad I did it."

"I am," Rainey said. "I've wanted to punch Cookie Kutter a time or two myself."

Cathleen laughed. "Her name is really Cookie Kutter? That isn't a joke?"

Rainey chuckled too. "Nope. That is what her parents named her."

Cathleen laughed louder.

"I know, right?" Rainey said.

In Rainey's estimation, Danny was trying to smooth over his retelling of one of Katie's least favorite memories when he said, "It wasn't really all that bad, Katie. I'm not so sure Cookie didn't overplay the moment for the camera."

Rainey chuckled. "Well, the blood was real."

Katie elbowed Rainey in the ribs. "There was no blood."

Rainey teased her. "Just a little drop, in the corner of Cookie's mouth. That was quite the right hook."

Katie playfully chucked Rainey's chin with her fist. "You should be careful then."

Rainey gave Katie's fist a quick kiss. "Always."

"Besides, I thought you were happy that video exists, so I can never run for any kind of political office," Katie said. "Can you imagine the airplay that one drunken moment would receive?"

Cathleen interjected, "You've forgotten who is in the White House. A squeaky clean past isn't necessarily a requirement for election anymore."

Danny mumbled something Rainey didn't catch but knew wasn't pleasant commentary on the current political atmosphere in DC.

Katie explained to Cathleen, "I don't want you to get the wrong impression. I'm not usually a violent person. There were mitigating circumstances. In addition to the alcohol, I was under many new stressors. I had recently recovered from a major trauma. I was taking hormone shots leading up to the procedure that produced the triplets. A crazed killer had put a severed head that looked a lot like me on the dock by our old house. I wasn't yet used to the constant threat of obsessed serial murderers lurking about."

Cathleen responded, "That sounds like a lot to deal with. I can understand your distress. I would have hit someone too."

Katie lifted her wine glass for a toast. "Well, no one has tried to kill one of us in almost two years. Things are looking up."

Cathleen indicated her compassion and knowledgeable understanding with her comment, "I'm sure the diligence weighs on you both."

Rainey changed the subject's tone with, "It's not so bad now that we have an exit plan."

Danny looked surprised. "An exit plan. Why don't I know these things?"

"It wouldn't be a good exit plan if people knew where we were going, now would it?"

"We decided to stop talking about it and make real plans to relocate if necessary." Katie laughed when she added, "It seems the moment we prepared for the worst, the danger subsided. I was kind of looking forward to waking up as strangers in a strange land."

Rainey hugged Katie to her side and said, "Even though you came up with the most excellent exit plan, be careful what you wish for."

Danny and Cathleen inclined out of their chairs to clink glasses with Rainey and Katie.

Danny said, "To exit plans and not having to use them."

Rainey watched as Danny added a smile meant for Cathleen and an extra clink of only their glasses. They leaned back into the cushions of the loveseat obviously sharing a secret.

Other than his mother, Rainey thought she probably knew Danny better than anyone else—until Cathleen. Twelve years his junior, an intelligence analyst with the National Security Agency, Danny's girlfriend was smart, and behind those hazel eyes, Rainey surmised, Cathleen was a tad playfully dangerous. She'd kept Danny interested for two years. That was a record.

Katie also had been paying attention and lacked Rainey's patience for an explanation. She asked, "What's up with you two?"

Danny seemed to ignore her question and asked one of his own, "I saw the "SOLD" sign on the house next door. Do you know who your new neighbors are going to be?"

"No, not yet. I think it sold yesterday," Katie said. "And you're ignoring my question."

Danny shifted his eyes to Rainey. "How about you? What do you know?"

She shrugged and answered, "I guess I'll find out when security tells me. I'm told my presence is part of the disclosure on the property, due to the multiple alarms and the body-dump several years back."

"Don't forget your mom shooting Gunny when she tried to kill you," Katie reminded.

Cathleen chuckled. "I'd say disclosure would be reasonable. It would certainly take the right kind of buyer knowing all of that."

Rainey caught the grin Danny was trying to conceal. She leaned forward and asked, "Did you quit, Danny? Are you coming to work with me?"

"You kept asking, and then Cathleen started looking at jobs down here too. One thing led to another. I'm officially done after we wrap up this Hale thing."

Katie sat up on the edge of her seat. "Danny, you bought the house next door!"

Danny answered, "Yes, we did, and she's agreed to marry me. Can you believe it?"

Katie jumped to her feet. "How absolutely wonderful."

In an instant, they were all standing and exchanging hugs.

Rainey hugged Cathleen and whispered, "Welcome to the family."

Katie was next. "I'm thrilled we're going to be neighbors. I'm dying to see inside that house. I missed the open house. I understand it's gorgeously modern."

"We love it. I took pictures this morning. They're on my..." Cathleen's words trailed off.

Rainey could not remember how many times she apologized already, but she did it again. "I'm so sorry about your phone. I think we recovered it from the bathtub in time and we put it in the rice right away."

Katie added, "I have no idea why that child is so obsessed with phones."

Cathleen did not appear upset. In fact, she never seemed flustered at all by much of anything.

She responded with a smile, "It was an accident. She didn't mean to drop it, and I should not have brought it with me to bath time. Lesson learned. Besides, if I can't recover the info from a waterlogged phone, I'm not very good at my job."

Katie hugged Cathleen again, saying, "I just love her, Danny. Nothing fazes her. We're going to need to knock a hole in the 'Great Wall of Rainey.' I mean really, don't you think that eighteen-inch thick brick fence is a bit much?"

Rainey cut off Katie's criticism of the fortress she built, asking Cathleen, "So, are you leaving NSA?"

"Officially, yes. Unofficially, I'm going to work in development with PBG in Research Triangle Park. We need more tools to combat hackers, so I'm going into the private sector to help build them." She smiled up at Rainey and said, "Bill Wise says to tell you, 'hello,' and it's time to go fishing with the kids again."

"I'll have to do that. Bill is a great guy. I think you'll enjoy working with him. You'll probably be working with Joey and Graham too. You met them at Molly's house on your last visit."

66

"Graham is the young man with you when Ellie Paxton tried to drown you in that lake, right?"

"Yes, that's him. He also wrote the program that found Ellie when she ran. He's different, but he's brilliant."

"Most programmers are," Cathleen said. "When Danny decided he was done with DC, I realized I didn't want to stay there without him. He suggested we come here and things fell into place."

Danny said, "We bid on the house sight unseen. We found out we got it yesterday."

Rainey raised her beer into the air. Danny and the others followed suit with their respective beverages.

"Cheers to good neighbors, lifelong friends, and having family close. Welcome home, you two."

When they relaxed back into their seats, Rainey asked, "What made you finally decide to leave, Danny? It wasn't just my asking you to work with me. What tipped the scale?"

"Alternative facts." He tilted his head back and sighed.

Katie sat up on the edge of her seat. "Yes! I wanted to throw something through the TV."

Danny stared up at the dark sky. A few stars winked through the wisps of clouds. The moon had a brown ring around it, foretelling of storms to come. No one said a word. All eyes were on Danny. He remained in the same posture as he finally began to speak.

"If only we knew then what we know now, only we did, and no one did a thing about it."

"We will never know it all, will we?" Katie asked.

Danny lowered his head and said, "No."

He then finished his beer in a long slow pull on the bottle. He stood and crossed to the refrigerator, grabbed another, and turned back to Rainey.

"You asked what finally did me in. It wasn't a case or a victim that tipped the scale. I found myself in a city filled with alternative truths that inspired a perpetual state of pondering what if…"

Rainey remembered that state of mind. She'd been there herself after the attack that almost took her life. She smiled at her friend and tipped her beer bottle in his direction. "Welcome to Bell-McNally Investigations. Where the only 'if' we have to ponder is if we're going to work from home or the office."

Danny twisted off the top of his beer and raised it for another toast.

"Let the mayhem begin."

#

"Junior has controlling interest in the bail business now. Mackie and I are not out fetching skippers, which pleases both of our respective spouses."

Rainey sat behind the desk in her home office. Seated across from her with a three-ring binder in his lap, Danny perused the case file created during the years Rainey followed Chance Hale's movements. Katie and Cathleen had long since gone to bed. While the future Bell-McNally investigators exchanged information on Hale, Rainey filled Danny in on the lives of the staff of Bell's Bail, with whom he soon would be sharing office space.

"Mackie is basically retired, which delights Thelma to no end. They bought an RV and are gone more than they are home these days."

Danny looked up from the binder to ask, "How's Ernie? Is she feeling better from that bout of pneumonia?"

"Ernie is excellent. That was a bit scary, but she's too mean to die," Rainey said, knowing if anything happened to that old woman it would devastate her. "She still comes to work two days a week, more out of boredom than need. She put away quite a retirement fund and does not need to work anymore. I do the billing for the consultant business, and Junior's wife handles the books for Bell's Bail."

"I'm glad to hear she's feeling better," Danny said, turning another page.

"She shows up on Tuesdays and Thursdays to help keep my schedule up to date and read through cases. Still playing gatekeeper, it works for both of us. As it turns out, Ernie has a knack for spotting overlooked little things in old case files, things dismissed as irrelevant that turn out to be important."

"That's a useful skill. Hey, I meant to ask you about Wendy. She sent me a letter, thanked me for the recommendation, but she withdrew her application to the Academy."

Rainey nodded, indicating that she knew. "After her kidnapping, she reevaluated what she wanted to do with the rest of her life. She wants to work with at risk kids."

"Is she quitting law enforcement?" Danny asked.

"No, she wants to stay in the department, but she'll be in juvenile crimes. Wendy said she wanted to help kids like Barron, not lock them up." Rainey smiled and added, "You know, she started the paperwork to officially adopt that kid."

"You seem pleased."

"I am. I'm proud of my sister. I'm proud of Barron too. He's doing great in school. You'll see him in the morning. He helps Wendy coach the triplets' soccer team."

"I can't wait to see them play this year. Has this age group progressed beyond just running around in circles or picking dandelions?"

Rainey chuckled. "Let's just say there are less of them wandering aimlessly about the field."

Danny reached for his notepad on the corner of the desk. He had been taking notes as he flipped through Rainey's old Chance Hale file.

He commented as he wrote, "I see here that Dr. Munzer identified the tool marks on the skull as coming from a bullhook, or ankus, or whatever you call that elephant prod."

"A goad," Rainey said. "It's an elephant goad. It's used to guide elephants. When used correctly and humanely, it keeps both keeper and animal safe. It took Munzer a while to find it. She took her grandkids to the circus, and it clicked. She spent a lot of time researching and talking to elephant managers until she found a closely matching example out of hundreds of customized bullhooks. This was long after Chance went to prison. He hasn't granted any interviews, so I don't know how a tool like that connects to him or Hale Trucking."

"Interesting choice of weapon. That has to be a major clue," Danny said, writing as he spoke.

"Yeah, it means something to this killer. They didn't find a bullhook in Chance's truck, but that accident scene was a mess, people everywhere, stuff scattered all over the road."

"Munzer says in her report that the 'hook is not really a hook.' What does she mean?"

"Look," Rainey said while bending a paperclip back and forth until she broke off a small section.

She worked it into a hook shape on one side and then jammed the still straight side into the eraser of a pencil. Rainey tapped the miniature hook against the desktop surface.

"It makes a linear mark when swung like this."

She began to reshape the hook.

"Now if I open this hook more and mold it like this, it looks like a squiggly, slightly bent cane handle. Now if I swing it at something, I will still get the linear wound, but this blunt end here will sink further into the skull. That's what she meant by 'not a hook.' "

Danny compared photos of the skulls sent to Quantico in the care of Rainey. There were six total, received by Dr. Munzer from January of 2000 to June of 2005.

"Okay," he said. "I see what she means. There is this puncture at the bottom of the wound, and the rest is a more crushing blow."

Rainey lifted a picture from her desk and held it out to Danny. "The same wound is on the skull found in Albemarle Sound. The teeth marks are there too."

"Did they ever figure out what those teeth belonged to?" Danny asked.

Rainey shook her head. "Munzer talked to wildlife experts. They all agreed that the animal that made them could have crushed the skull. Instead, it played with it, gnawed on it. They were sure the teeth marks were non-aggressive in nature, like a dog chewing a bone. What they couldn't agree on was the species of animal that made the marks. Black bear and mountain lion received the most votes."

"Shouldn't it be easy to distinguish between those two?"

Rainey explained, "Munzer said the teeth marks weren't normal. The experts thought maybe the bite had been changed due to injury."

"Lions and bears and elephant goads," Danny said. "There isn't much normal about this case. And to add to that, I'm going to agree with you. I don't think Joshua Hale did any of these first four murders. I believe there might be more than one serial murderer in this family. The frozen lake murder victims had slightly different head wounds, but the freezing is the same, the knots are the same. Tying that knot in the packaging of the bones delivered to Quantico screams compulsory linkage."

"I always wanted to lay a piece of rope on the table in front of Chance Hale, just to see how compulsive his rope fetish is. But I've never had the opportunity to thoroughly interview him. A guardian or Blackman always seemed to swoop in to protect him."

"Speaking of Blackman, did you hear back from Molly?"

"Hang on, I'll look." Rainey checked her email.

Horace Blackman had been Molly Kincaid's mentor and former law partner. Blackman's Law Firm became Kincaid Law Firm. Rainey had sent an email to Molly, her closest friend since leaving the BAU and sometime client, asking about conflict of interest.

"Okay, yes, here we go. Molly says there is no conflict of interest. She checked the firm's records. Apparently, Blackman handled Chance's legal woes off the books, for whatever reason. There were no records linking the law firm to Chance or Hale Trucking."

Danny put his pen down and considered Rainey for a few seconds. "Do you think you could be wrong about Hale? He was in prison when Vanessa Wilhelm's remains turned up in that crab pot contraption in the sound."

Rainey pointed at the binder in Danny's lap. "There is too much circumstantial evidence for him not to be involved in some way. He's either a stone cold killer or he knows one. I stand by that judgment."

"Wood believed you too," Danny said. "This case put you in the BSU training program. That says a lot about Wood's confidence in your abilities and the case you built."

"Remind me to thank Chance for my career break." Rainey thought for a second, and then asked, "Why does he want to see me, Danny?"

"Hale is scheduled for release next week. Florida has hinted they may prosecute him for a murder from 2000. That, coupled with the body found in his old North Dakota home may have been motivating factors in his asking to see you now. I think the uncertainty may have driven him to manipulate the situation. His defense already suggested you tampered with evidence. This might be an attempt to implicate you further or to find out what we know."

"And this will be his first interview since he entered prison?" Rainey asked and then qualified the question. "I just assumed he'd consent left and right to gain an audience for his persecuted-innocent act."

"The BAU sent him a request for an interview every year he's been incarcerated. We sent requests to his remaining family members and people who worked closely with Joshua Hale. We never received a positive response from anyone."

"No employees would talk to me either. That company had a cult vibe. Does it still exist?"

Danny shook his head and began flipping back through his notes, as he spoke. "No. Hang on. Okay, here it is. Hale Trucking dissolved in 2010. Up to that point, Robby Hughes ran it, at least on paper. Slowly, a stockholder named Jean Berry bought Robby and Chance out, loaning them money against their shares. Easy picking it would seem. Hale Trucking was dissolved and absorbed by a Löwenherz Industries, LLC."

"I met Jean Berry. She was the office manager."

Danny looked up from his notepad. "Ms. Berry managed those two boys and took the family business by being an opportunistic loan shark. She sold off the land and equipment and cashed out with a hefty retirement fund."

"Good for her," Rainey said. "So, Chance is getting out next week."

"He thinks he is, anyway. When Chance contacted us last week, consenting to an interview but stipulating you come along, we had to ask you. I think he relied on that. So, we specified that if he wants to talk to you, he has to let us listen. Whether he is a son of a serial killer or an actual serial murderer himself, either way, the BAU wants to know what went on in that family."

"Well, his genetics is undoubtedly interesting, to say the least," Rainey offered.

Danny nodded in agreement. "I don't think I've seen a more twisted family tree before."

"No kidding," Rainey agreed and then asked, "What's going on with the DNA from the remains they found behind the wall in North Dakota?"

71

"I'm not sure," Danny said. "I'll check on that tomorrow."

Rainey turned her attention to the computer screen and scrolled through more of Chance's prison records.

A few quiet minutes went by while they both read, until Rainey asked, "Is this a legit suicide attempt, or was he drug seeking that first year in prison?"

"Well, he stabbed himself in the neck with a pen. Whether it was a suicide or not, it definitely warranted intervention." Danny paused and looked up at Rainey. He chuckled, as he said, "You know, they made him use crayons for years after that."

Rainey smiled back at Danny. He had relaxed since arriving and seemed closer to the person with whom she had spent more late nights than with her slumbering spouse upstairs. She saw his dimple deepen with the simultaneous unspoken realization that they were once again a formidable team. They held the eye contact long enough to prompt knowing nods from both of them before Danny lowered his gaze to the binder in his lap.

Rainey refocused on the computer screen with the comment, "Did he do his homework in pastels?"

They both laughed and returned to reading until Rainey said, "Hale committed vehicular homicide, and for that, he received residential drug rehabilitation, mental health counseling, two four-year college degrees, and eight years of three hots and a cot. Sounds like a better deal that student loans. And what are these special skills that keep him at Butner instead of back in Florida?"

Danny looked up from his note taking. "His degrees are in Design and Mechanical Engineering. He worked with a manufacturer to redesign a medical device used in oncology. That's my understanding."

Rainey read from the computer screen, "He can 'fix stuff.' That's what it says here. Engineering fits well with his OCD diagnosis."

Danny pointed his pen toward Rainey's monitor. "If you look at his disciplinary sheet, it's clean except for one incident when the contraband sweep officers tossed his cell," Danny used air quotations around the concluding adverb, "aggressively."

Rainey nodded. "I see he had his resulting solitary time reduced by a Dr. Janzen."

"He's a psychiatrist. He went to bat for Chance. He told the COs to knock it off and petitioned for special consideration of Chance's OCD diagnosis. I've noticed nothing in your notes about his obsessive behavior before he went to prison. Do you think he's acting?"

"The alcohol and drugs must have masked his obsessive compulsive nature when I was watching him. And remember, I actually spent very little time with him."

Danny agreed, "He was definitely self-medicating. According to the prison staff, his compulsory behaviors grew much worse once he was sober. Learning to cope with it is part of his ongoing rehabilitation treatment plan."

Rainey asked, "Why is he in the cancer ward?"

Danny answered, "Inmate Hale had a melanoma removed, according to his records. That's all I have access to at the moment. I'll need a warrant to access his other medical records or his consent, which he has been reluctant to give."

"Well, if he's dying, I hope he's ready to help close these cases."

Danny knew her well. He said, "I hope he's ready to come clean about Alyson Grayson. I know you desperately want to tell her mother what happened to her."

Rainey had carried the heavy albatross of her promise to Alyson's mother for nearly twenty years, but never fully understood what that promise meant until she had children of her own.

Rainey looked across the desk at Danny and quoted a familiar Coleridge poem, The Rime of the Ancient Mariner, "Since then, at an uncertain hour, that agony returns. And till my ghastly tale is told, this heart within me burns."

12

March 25, 2017
Homestead Park
Chapel Hill, NC

"In the age six and under group, youth soccer is less about the game itself, and more about one or two gifted athletes in the bunch being casually followed about inside a delineated area until someone says the snacks are ready."

Cathleen replied to Katie's comment, "Oh, I think they're precious. And look at your three. They are tearing it up out there."

"Weather, no hitting," Wendy King said, as Weather took a swing at the kid who had just tackled her to the ground.

Wendy turned to her half-sister, "Rainey, I'm going to have to pull her out if she does that again."

Weather ran after the ball and was immediately tackled from behind by the same kid. She jumped up this time and planted both palms in his chest, sending him back onto his butt.

Rainey said to Wendy. "If you don't go get her, I will. That's enough of little Miss Cloudy today."

Katie stepped up to Rainey's side and asked, "What's up with her lately."

Barron, Wendy's foster child, spoke up, "The diva is feeling shade from somewhere."

Rainey chuckled and wrapped her arm around Barron's shoulder. "I love this kid. You are so damn clever."

Wendy came back with Weather and a red card. "She's out for the day. Watch your back. Daddy's pissed over there." She indicated with her head the man shouting at the officials.

Katie asked, "Is the kid hurt?"

Wendy pushed a substitute onto the field. This one's shin guards were so loose on his tiny stick legs that they shifted from side to side as he ran out into the fray.

She answered Katie, "No, only his dad's pride seems injured. A girl made his boy cry. You know the type."

Rainey intercepted Weather on her way to the bench. "Let's go, grumpy. We need to have a chat."

"Watch the boys, Mom," Katie said to her mother, Melanie Meyers, and then followed Rainey and Weather to a private spot in the park.

"Watch my back," Rainey whispered as she passed Danny.

Rainey glanced back over her shoulder at the dad, who was still ranting at the official. Some parents were a bit too invested in their kid's sports activities. This guy apparently fit the mold. Rainey decided to focus on her own child and hope the red-faced man would calm down soon.

Rainey watched Weather stomp behind her mother, arms crossed, untied ribbon trailing from her hair. A trained behaviorist, Rainey had interviewed many criminals, but her own child presented her biggest challenge to date. By the time they sat down in the grass, Weather's bottom lip stuck out like a diving board, and her attitude had worsened.

Katie said to the steaming little being, "Weather, we can't let you play with the others if you continue hitting."

"Nee Nee hits bad people."

The feelings evoked by Katie's expression when she locked eyes with Rainey felt like condemnation with a bit of self-righteousness on the side.

"Well, Rainey Blue, I'm leaving this to you," she said. She stood and patted Weather on the head. "Honey, Nee Nee is going to explain her behavior to you. I'm going to go watch your brothers. I love you. No more hitting, okay?"

"Okay, Mommy," Weather said, now wearing an absolutely angelic smile.

Once Katie cleared the area, Rainey said, "Hey, you. What's up with throwing me under the bus?"

"I can't throw you, Nee Nee. You're too heavy."

"That's true. Anyway, when have you seen me hit people?"

"On the punching bag. You pretend to hit bad people. When you are mad, you hit them harder."

Rainey recalled Weather asking who she was talking to when she said, "Take that," after a long session on the heavy bag. She had responded to Weather's inquiry, "Bad people," without giving it much thought. That should never be the case when dealing with Weather. A lesson Rainey repeatedly learned with her baby girl.

"You are very observant for a five-year-old, young lady, and smarter than the average bear."

"I'm not a bear," Weather said, giggling.

Rainey snatched the child into her arms and snuggled her through that smelly kid odor.

"Pew, you stink like a dirty kid."

"I am a dirty kid," Weather said, soaking up the hugs and one on one time each child craved.

As parents of triplets, they did their best to give them individualized attention every day. Rainey loved the uniqueness of her children, each with their distinct gifts and issues. Mack was a natural athlete. His only fears seemed to revolve around being left alone, a remnant from an unfortunate trauma while bearing witness to his Aunt Wendy's kidnapping. Rainey marveled at the core strength and agility the biggest of her boys possessed. He loved gymnastics class and the climbing wall. She assumed he'd climb mountains some day. Katie recently caught him attempting to scale the brick wall around the yard. They now regretted the design decision of roughly finished bricks jutting out randomly along the otherwise toehold-lacking surface. Mack's parental challenge required they try to instill some caution without dampening his sense of adventure.

Timothy, with a slighter build, ran like the wind, but he was not much of a sports enthusiast. He tumbled, played soccer and basketball, and was generally good at all three, but he only participated because his siblings did. Timothy's passions lay in the world of insects and animals. He also loved music and could plunk out tunes of his own making on the piano. It was not Mozart, but it didn't give Rainey a headache the non-musical triplets did when they banged on the keys. Timothy was the quiet, shy, introspective one of the three. He loved everyone, but his love for his dog surpassed all others. The parental challenge with him involved not allowing his siblings' huge personalities to overshadow Timothy's more Zen existence.

Weather was, as Danny described her, the mastermind. This little person had intrigued Rainey since she discovered her daughter's manipulative powers within days of her birth. Katie's mini-me sized up situations and people quickly. Rainey often watched Weather work the crowd at family gatherings. Though her challenges were many, focused in the right places, this girl child's self-confidence and unbending-will would resist anyone throwing up barriers to her goals.

Pound for pound, Weather was also the most gifted athlete in the bunch. Quick, with extraordinary hand-eye coordination for her age group, Weather loved to play all kinds of sports. Her issues with organized team activities stemmed from a competitive streak that clouded her judgment at times. It bothered Katie more than Rainey, who saw her daughter's desire to win as a positive trait that needed honing. Rainey had worked in an extremely competitive field, especially for women. She was sure Weather's rejection of defeat would be a future asset, and her willingness to fight was not such a bad thing either.

"Look, I know getting knocked down isn't fun, but you can't hit players for trying to get the ball from you."

"Can you pinch them?" Weather asked.

"No, honey. You aren't supposed to intentionally hurt players."

"Then he should have a red card too. He pinched me, and it hurt. He did it two times."

Weather yanked up her shirt, exposing her torso. Rainey saw two small, but intensely black and blue bruises on her daughter's side.

"Is that why you hit him?" Rainey asked, already rising to her feet.

"Yes. He isn't supposed to do that, and it hurt."

From the color of the bruising, Rainey was sure it had hurt. Impressed with Weather's instinct to fight back rather than cry and run to find her mother, Rainey lifted the child into her arms.

"I'm sorry that happened, honey. If any player does something like this, please come tell Wendy or me. What he did was wrong, but you still cannot hit anyone during the games."

"But he pinched me hard," Weather argued.

"Your coach and the officials are in charge of making sure he doesn't pinch you. You have to tell them so they can do their jobs."

"Okay, Nee Nee."

"If those kids weren't raised by dykes, maybe they'd learn some manners."

The raging father of the offending pincher was closing fast on Rainey and Weather. Rainey put her daughter on the ground and whispered in her ear, "Run to Danny." She could see Danny heading her way. He extended his arms and collected Weather up from the ground. By this time, a large part of the Bell-Meyers entourage watched the angry dad close on her position.

Rainey turned to face the much larger man with the red face and fire in his eyes.

"I'm sorry, did you say something?"

The man barged into her space, breathing down on her like a predatory animal. "That little miniature dyke better keep her hands to herself."

Weather was correct. Her Nee Nee did want to hit the bad man. Instead, she said, "Sir, this escalation isn't necessary, nor is it appropriate in front of all these children. If you'd care to walk over to the picnic area and have a calm discussion, I'd be happy to accompany you."

The man stepped closer, glared down at her, and uttered his threat, "I'll whip her ass and yours too if she touches my kid again."

Every fiber of Rainey's being wanted to leg whip this guy to the ground, twist his arm behind his back, and put a knee on his spine, while she whispered in his ear about the ass kicking he was about to receive. She resisted, but she didn't back down either.

"Sir, my child has deep black bruises where your son pinched her. Now, kids will be kids. I've dealt with my child's reactionary behavior to your son's assault. If you remind him that pinching isn't part of the game, I think we're done here."

This guy was in such a rage, he wasn't listening to Rainey. He glared at her and inched forward, puffing out his chest.

"They shouldn't let you people near kids anyway," he thundered. "I can't wait 'til they start lining you up for the ovens."

In her peripheral vision, Rainey saw Danny give Weather to Katie and begin walking toward them. Rainey held her hand out by her hip, signaling Danny to stop. She did not back away from the threatening man. She leaned even closer. So close, she could see his nose hairs.

She said in a calm, quiet voice, "Sir, I just finished talking to my child about the proper way to evaluate and react to a threat. Maybe you could do with some risk assessment training yourself."

"That's not a threat. It's a promise I voted for, and I aim to see they keep it. You sick fucks need to be eradicated from society."

Rainey smiled up at the seething man. "You have failed to assess the danger you are in currently."

The man raised his voice even louder, as he was now drawing more attention to the standoff. "Oh, I'm in danger, am I? What, are the politically correct homo police going to come tell me to leave the faggots alone?"

Rainey lowered her voice even more. "Sir, I'm not going to get into a physical confrontation with you over a child's soccer game. What I will do is a favor for you." She turned and pointed at Danny whom Cathleen had now joined. "See those two, they are federal agents. See that woman over there that looks like a younger version of me, she's a deputy sheriff. I'm retired FBI. If you put your hands on me now, I'm sure they will be happy to testify to the Justice Department about your hate crime. Go home, sir. Cool off. And gain some perspective."

"Oh, so I've run up on one of Killary's nasty women. You go high, I'll go low, cunt. Trump's in office now. There's no such thing as a hate crime."

Slowly, Rainey became aware that the game had stopped and a crowd of people closed in on her and the fuming man. She heard one voice say, "No hate, not here," and then another. Soon an entire chorus encircled them with chants of "No hate, not here." People stepped close and then in between Rainey and Mr. Make America Great Again, creating a barrier of chanters.

"No hate, not here."

Not finding any supporters, the man backed away slowly. The chanters followed him all the way to the parking lot. His discomfort was evident when he drove away leaving his son on the sidelines crying. Rainey held her breath, as she watched Katie and Weather walk toward the boy. Weather spoke to him and gave him a hug.

Danny was suddenly at Rainey's side. "Now, that gives us hope for the future."

Rainey laughed, "Which part? Me not taking him down right here in front of all these people and the kids, or Weather playing peacemaker?"

Danny chuckled. "I'd say it's a little bit of both."

Katie waited for an adult to claim the child before she returned with Weather. Halfway to where Rainey stood, Katie was joined by a woman she obviously knew. Rainey watched their greeting out of habit. When a stranger bee-lined for someone she loved, it drew her attention. Katie silenced any warning bells when she gave the woman a hug. Still, it felt odd to see someone in big sunglasses on an overcast day. Befitting the remainder of her bohemian Hollywood starlet incognito-style, an oversized scarf covered her head and draped casually over her shoulders. One lone brunette curl graced her forehead.

Katie introduced the woman as they walked up. "Rainey, this is Ann Burke, with Tiny Hart Living."

Rainey recognized the name from emails exchanged with the contractor Katie hired to design and build four tiny houses for the women's shelter. Katie hoped to buy more land and open more spaces for women and children needing safe and affordable housing. This was Katie's project and she'd tackled it almost entirely on her own. Rainey had been involved only so far as to address some safety concerns about egress and bullet resistance. After all, these women were fleeing dangerous domestic violence situations. Bullets could definitely be in play. As one of the women at the shelter said while looking over the plans, "Man, that's like shooting fish in a barrel. Unless that's armor plating, I'm not locking myself in there with him out here shooting through the walls."

Ann wafted forward bringing with her the scents of burning sage and essential oils. Her voice floated smooth like old whiskey, deep and raspy, when she extended her hand to Rainey.

"Oh, I just add the finishing touches. My husband, Hart—that's his name—does the contractor part. He really does 'put a lot of heart in our tiny homes.'" Ann put air quotation marks around the slogan.

Rainey remembered seeing that phrase on the emails she exchanged with Hart Burke, Ann's husband.

Ann grabbed Rainey's hand and patted it, while saying, "I feel like I should know you, with all the emailing back and forth. It is a pleasure to finally meet you in person, Rainey, even if it is surrounded by so much negative energy. That man is a highly unpleasant entity."

Rainey agreed, "Yes, he is."

"Are you coming with us to procure oddities and art that speaks to women?" Ann asked.

Katie answered for Rainey, "No, sadly my justice warrior has an interview with an inmate up at Butner."

Rainey was thinking she wouldn't be going to procure anything today. Given her choice, she'd be relaxing on a couch watching games featuring the last eight teams standing in the NCAA basketball tournament.

"Oh, that sounds interesting. Exploring the criminal mind. Oddities of a different sort, I suppose," Ann said.

Rainey chuckled at Ann's eccentric wit and responded, "You could say that."

Ann finally let go of Rainey's hand, as she said, "Well, I am looking forward to you seeing the houses. Your contributions to safety will go in all of our homes from now on."

Rainey smiled at Ann and said, "That's good to hear. Multiple egresses from what amounts to a large box are important. Keeping people out is great, but getting out when they want to keep you in is imperative as well."

Before Ann could comment, Wendy walked up leading her nephews. "Well, they called the game." She bumped into Rainey, like the little sister she was. "I can't take you anywhere."

"He was a bad man, Wendy," Weather said, "but Nee Nee did not hit him. She used her words." She looked up at Rainey beaming and giving her the thumbs up. "Good job, Nee Nee."

"Thank you, honey. Weather, show Wendy where that boy pinched you," Rainey said.

Weather pulled her shirt up to proudly show off her wounds, explaining, "He said he was sorry. I said I was sorry too."

Rainey smiled at Weather. "That is great. Good job."

Katie laughed. "They'll probably end up dating, and this will all be some funny story we tell to embarrass them."

Rainey wasn't amused at the prospects of the kid's dad ever being a part of their lives. She shook off the thought and said to Wendy, "I told her to bring it to your attention if that happens again."

Wendy bent to kiss Weather's cheek. "I got your back, kid."

Weather ran off to chase her brothers.

Rainey said to Wendy, "I'd appreciate it if you told the officials about the pinching. Just so they're aware of her motivation to react. I don't want her reputation to get out of hand at age five."

Wendy laughed. "I will, but I don't think any scouts were in the stands today."

Rainey shook her head. "Smartass."

Katie slid her arm around Rainey's waist.

Rainey asked, "Did she show you those pinches?"

"Yes, and she's done worse to her brothers, so don't reward her too much with sympathy." Katie rose on her tiptoes to kiss Rainey's cheek. "Okay, mom is taking the kids to her house. Cathleen, Ann, and I are going shopping for tiny house accessories. We'll see you late this evening, right?"

"Probably. I can't really give you a time."

Katie smiled and gave Rainey a peck on the lips.

"I'll see you when I see you then. You be safe, Rainey Blue Bell."

Rainey smiled and hugged Katie close, saying, "Always."

13

All prisons have one thing in common. If observed from a satellite image, even when the fences are impossible to see, it is still easy to ascertain where the boundaries are. The same primordial desire for freedom that pushes an animal to walk a recognizable path around the perimeter of its pen drives humans around the prison yard. Geronimo walked a shallow ditch into the hard clay of the enclosure where he spent his final days. The drive for freedom lives in all the creatures on the earth, even those that should never experience it again.

Rainey turned off the longleaf pine-lined Old Oxford Road into the crown jewel of the Federal Bureau of Prisons. During World War II, Camp Butner had been a US Army installation situated on the dividing line between the North Carolina counties of Durham and Granville. Mostly a training facility and hospital, part of the camp had been used to hold German prisoners of war. Today, another type of prisoner accommodation replaced part of old Camp Butner—the Butner Federal Correctional Complex. With three institutions housing low to medium security inmates and an additional medical facility handling all security levels, the inmate population ranged from those in need of special medical care to the extremely mentally disturbed.

Home of the largest medical facility in the Federal Bureau of Prisons, Butner handled a comprehensive array of medical problems, specializing in oncology and behavioral science. John Hinckley, Jr. spent time in Butner. The prison is home to Wall Street fraudster Bernie Madoff and probably will be for the remainder of his days. Frank Calabrese, Jr., hit man for the Chicago Outfit Mafia, died in Butner. Some, like Russell Weston, Jr., responsible for the US Capital shooting in 1998, judged too mentally ill for trial and too dangerous for the street remain incarcerated at Butner on an indefinite basis. On this cloudy Saturday afternoon, an inmate waited for his scheduled visitors in the oncology wing.

Rainey and Danny made their way down the glaringly white hallway of the medical center, guided by a uniformed correctional officer. The United States Public Health Service Commissioned Corps officers walked the halls in uniforms resembling those of the US Navy, white shirts, and dark pants, with rank epaulets on their shoulders and chests full of ribbons. These healthcare and medical personnel were members of one of the lesser known of the seven uniformed services of the United States. Nurses passed dressed in the official uniform, only gave away their professions with a belt of accessories at their waists.

The hallway smelled and looked like any other hospital. In case Rainey should forget where she was, she listened beyond the beeps and bleeps, under the hushed voices, where the institution lived. There she heard the occasional slap and drag rhythm of leg restraints against the floor, the jingle of waist chains, the clank of a heavy metal door closing them in, her in. Rainey felt the familiar quickening of her innate being's recognition of being locked inside with thousands of males. No female animal faces that knowledge without a wee bit of panic. Rainey's training required she focus that fear into heightened awareness.

She glanced at Danny, as they strode side by side behind their guide. "I forgot how this feels," she said.

"What do you mean?"

"It's been a while since I've been surrounded by this much testosterone. I think I can actually smell it under the antiseptic. It's like mouthwash and male musk became an air-freshener."

They passed under a sign marked "Pharmacy" where rows of chemotherapy bags hung on the other side of the window. The inmates housed here were thinking less about the bars and razor wire outside and more about surviving cancer on the inside.

Lieutenant Holmes, who rarely commented throughout his escort duty from the front gate, spoke as they passed the pharmacy. "They get better care here than most would get on the outside. Some of them are lucky they landed in here. Law abiding citizens die every day without treatment."

"Prison might be the only healthcare option for a lot of people in the near future," Danny commented, with an unmistakably hostile tone. "Five years for burglary and free cancer treatment sounds inviting to the hopeless."

"This isn't Club Med," their escort replied.

Danny fired back quickly, "It's better than club dead."

Rainey thought to herself that Danny may still have his federal credentials, but he had long since lost the bipartisan objectivity required to carry them. He seemed to forget where he was and what he represented. FBI agents aren't allowed to have opinions about politics publicly, especially not in the current climate and certainly not in a federal facility. Rainey recognized the bitterness and hoped it passed quickly for him. Danny blamed his disdain for his job on the current administration. Rainey suspected the toll nearly fifteen years submerged in the depravity of BAU investigations had a hand in it too. Rainey was thankful now that she got out when she did before it did irreparable damage. She wasn't so sure Danny had made it out in time.

"Lieutenant Holmes," Rainey said to their escort, "how long has Hale been in this wing?"

She knew she couldn't ask about Chance's diagnosis or treatment, but she wanted to distract the officer who, at the moment, eyed Danny suspiciously.

"Inmate Hale came to Butner Medical to recover from a suicide attempt shortly after his incarceration in Florida in 2010. He was admitted to the addiction recovery program, which he completed successfully in December of 2012."

"What's his prognosis? Are we looking at a dying man's confession today?" Danny was more direct and seemingly over his unprofessional conduct for the moment.

"Inmate Hale doesn't have cancer."

Rainey stopped walking, which caused the two men to halt as well.

She asked, "Then why are we meeting in the oncology wing?"

"Hale is a trustee assigned to this ward. This is where he is during visiting hours, so this is where you are. May we continue, ma'am?"

Rainey couldn't decide if Lieutenant Holmes's tone was condescending or if he simply lacked congeniality, but since she was inside his facility and Danny was being an ass, she chose to ignore the tenor of contempt in his voice.

"Yes, please. Lead on."

The lieutenant led them to a private room with a sign reading "Medical Consultation" on the door. Two armchairs had been placed on one side of a large desk, with a single wingback leather chair facing them from the other side. Medical diagrams lined the walls—illustrations of skeletal structure and muscle groups, the liver, heart, testicles, and other organs where cancer might lurk. An x-ray viewing box hung on the wall over the desk. In the corner, two dog-eared file boxes labeled "C. O. Hale Legal Docs" in fading black block letters waited for their namesake.

After showing Danny and Rainey into the room, Holmes said, "I'll go get inmate Hale," and closed the door behind him.

Rainey turned to Danny immediately upon hearing the click of the door latch.

"Hey, I know you're done with being a Fed and all that, but we need those credentials and institutional cooperation to conduct this interview. Can you chill out on the attitude a bit?"

Danny countered with, "Did you see that '88' tattoo on his wrist when he reached for the gate? What does that tell you?"

"It tells me that we are in North Carolina, the home of NASCAR, and despite white supremacists use of the number '88' to represent 'Heil Hitler,' in this case I'm going to go with he's a Dale Jr. fan."

"Why give him the benefit of the doubt? You're getting soft, Bell."

Rainey smiled at him, before explaining, "Maybe because I saw a truck in the parking lot with the license plate 'LTHOLMES,' Dale Jr. stickers on the back window, and a number '88' flag on the antenna. Don't call me soft. Just catch up, McNally."

Danny chuckled and said, "I should know to never doubt you."

Rainey laughed with him. "Remember that."

The surliness left Danny's demeanor. He offered a mea culpa, "Sorry about the snark. I'll keep it to a minimum."

Keys jangled outside the door. The knob turned and in walked Chance Obadiah Hale, unshackled and completely free to lunge for Rainey's throat. When his hand came toward her, she instinctively flinched and reached for the Glock absent from her side. She and Danny had locked away their weapons and phones in her car trunk gun safe before entering the prison. After the instinctual reaction, Rainey relaxed her hands to her side.

"I'm not shaking your hand."

Chance smiled and dropped his extended arm.

"I understand your reluctance to shake the hand of a man you suspect is a serial killer. I don't blame you."

Rainey chuckled, giving no weight to his platitudes, which she suspected were total bullshit.

"Oh, don't take it personally, Chance. Some of you guys like to play with yourselves before coming to an interview and get off on shaking hands with a dick-stained grip. I'd rather not share the love if you know what I mean."

Lieutenant Holmes escorted his prisoner to the other side of the table, where he seated Chance in the leather wingback chair—the power position in the room. Holmes held out handcuffs.

"Would you be more comfortable if he were cuffed? He isn't generally in restraints."

Chance added, "I didn't ask you here to harm you Supervisory Special Agent Bell. I saw in a publication that you had acquired a new title sometime back. You were always so ambitious."

The dimple between Lieutenant Holmes' eyes deepened, as he silently questioned Chance's use of Rainey's former title. As far as Holmes knew, she was a private citizen escorted into his facility by an FBI agent. Rainey waved off the cuffs and took a seat in one of the armchairs across the table from Chance, without responding to the lieutenant's unanswered question. She did not mind confusing him a bit. He had been condescending to her. Rainey thought he deserved a few minutes of wondering who she really was.

The lieutenant put away his handcuffs and moved toward the door.

"I'll be right outside," he said.

Rainey began speaking as soon as the door closed. "I'm no longer a federal agent, but you knew that, Chance. The flattery is new from you, but at least you've learned some decorum. Since we've known each other so long, you can call me Rainey. I'm just plain ol' citizen Rainey now."

"I'm sorry, old habit. I read that you were nearly killed and then left the BAU. Sorry about that, too. You were a good agent, despite trying to hang multiple murders on me."

"Life is good. Don't worry about me," Rainey responded dismissively.

He was watching her, hoping his successful manipulation of this meeting would be rewarded with her gratitude. She gave Chance no indication that she wanted to be there, that she had waited for his confession for nineteen years. Rainey may have desired another crack at Chance Hale, but she would never let him think she was grateful for his time. Danny sat down beside Rainey, drawing Chance's attention.

"And you must be Supervisory Special Agent Daniel McNally. You are just as you have been described—a big Irish fellow. I was told you were the conduit to this meeting with Agent, I mean Rainey. Thank you."

Danny nodded at Chance and pulled a small recorder from the inside breast pocket of his jacket. He placed it on the table and pushed the record button, before replying coldly, "State the date, your full name, current location, and acknowledge you are aware of being recorded."

Chance showed no annoyance and responded politely, "I am aware this meeting is being recorded and give my consent. My name is Chance Obadiah Hale, and I am a current resident at Butner Federal Correctional Complex, in Butner, North Carolina. Today's date is March 25, 2017."

Danny continued, "You can call me Agent McNally. We won't ever be on a first name basis. Unlike former Agent Bell, I'm still in the Bureau and must inform you of your rights. You have the right to…"

While Danny reminded Chance of his rights, Rainey studied her old foe. Chance was no longer a lanky drunk trying to recover. Along with the apparent changes in his vocabulary skills, his self-confidence and demeanor improved with his education and sobriety. For the first time in any of their interactions, Chance was making and holding eye contact with the people in the room. A lot had changed about him, but not Rainey's suspicions.

She could see the scar over his right eye. Rainey knew about permanent scars and how every look in the mirror reminded Chance of the vehicular homicide that landed him in prison. At thirty-five years old and off illegal drugs and sober for the last eight years, Chance's muscles had thickened. He appeared to work out and looked healthy. With clear skin and a blush in his cheeks, prison life had been good to him it seemed. His long hair gone, Chance now wore it trimmed close to his scalp. His once sun-bleached, almost white, hair had darkened to the color of wet sand. The scraggly patches of beard on his jaw and chin were gone. He was clean-shaven and wearing wire-rimmed glasses. He looked more the studious professional than his former beach bum manifestation.

She realized both men were looking at her.

"What?"

"Identify your voice for the record," Danny said.

"Rainey Bell, formerly with the FBI and now a private citizen. By the way, nice touch suggesting we meet on the cancer ward. Did you pretend to be dying so I'd rush to get your final confession?"

Chance smiled. "Always so suspicious of my motives. I assure you, this is better than the interrogation rooms in my old unit. I wanted us to be comfortable. You look great, by the way; a little age and less hair, but still a looker. The woman in black style works for you too, especially the boots and the long duster. You look like you stepped out of a graphic novel, or no, wait, Barbara Stanwyck in that black leather outfit galloping around the Big Valley."

He avoided her question by fishing for a compliment on the new and improved Chance Hale. Rainey didn't take the bait. She knew he would spend as much time tearing her down as complimenting her, the moment he thought she cared what he had to say. Rainey always suspected a skillful manipulator lurked beneath the veneer of the maladroit persona she knew before today. Education, no booze or drugs, and regular meals gave Chance the opportunity to explore this new Mr. Enlightenment guise. Chance Hale 2.0 projected concern for others. That was a change, but it didn't negate his overwhelming concern for himself. Rainey hid that she noticed anything but the most obvious differences.

"You wear glasses," she stated flatly, attaching no emotion to the revelation. It was only a fact.

Glaring at Chance and with a glaze of contempt on his words, Danny played bad cop and said, "There is no 'us' that includes you. There's you, the convicted murderer, and us, the people leaving here soon if you don't get to the point."

Chance ignored Danny's bravado like the experienced convict he was and refocused on Rainey. "Thank you for coming. I'm sure you are wondering why I asked to see you."

"Could it be the skeleton discovered in the Albemarle Sound last August? Or maybe the unidentified body they found in your old North Dakota home? Could it be you're preparing for a parole hearing? Whatever it is, talking to me gets you nothing. I have no law enforcement ties or influence. Or have you finally decided to come clean about Alyson?"

Chance leaned back deeper into the chair. He seemed to be searching Rainey's expression for clues as to how to play her. He opened his mouth to speak.

"I—"

Having seen him measuring her intent, Rainey cut him off. She did not project anger. Her words, measured and delivered flatly, addressed only the facts. Her lack of emotional investment in their relationship would be far more unsettling to Chance.

"I came here because it is the only way you would consent to an interview with the Behavioral Analysis Unit. I believe, as I always have, you know what happened to Alyson. You have carried a secret with you all these years. Look where you ended up. I am not here because you asked to see me. I came because one day you are going to tell what you know about Alyson Grayson's disappearance. Maybe that's today."

Chance calmly responded, "I know I was less than cooperative about Alyson. I was a punk kid. I was too drunk and high to remember anything beyond her giving me a ride home. I always hoped my brain would one day spit out what happened. I am sorry to say it has not. I can't provide you or Alyson's family with answers."

Rainey listened to Chance and waited to take control. He wanted her there. That was the only power she held over him today. Once he had finished claiming innocence in Alyson's case, Rainey stood.

"Then you have nothing to say that is of interest to me."

Chance reached for the breast pocket of his prison issue khaki-brown shirt. Danny reacted, standing immediately.

"Hands on the table!"

Chance left the tip of a piece of paper peeking from his pocket and returned his hands to the table.

"You two really need to relax. I'm not about to ruin my chances of getting out of here. I want to show Rainey the email I received today."

Rainey was skeptical. "How do you have access to email?"

Chance explained, "I work on the chemo pumps. I collaborated with the manufacturer on a modification to improve the pump's design. I maintain most of the equipment in this unit. I have access to a maintenance department computer. Check with the COs."

Danny assured him, "I will."

"I'm going to get written up for this email account, but I think it's important that you see this."

Rainey smirked at Chance. "Oh, so you're martyring yourself for my benefit. You know, by now I would have thought you'd understand, I don't believe most of what comes out of your mouth."

Chance indicated the paper poking out of his pocket with his chin and his eyes, not daring to move his hands again.

"It came from the dead woman's account, the one they found in the Albemarle Sound. It isn't the first threat I've received. Trace the email and find whoever sent it. I am pretty sure it's the killer who has stalked me my entire life."

Danny reached over the desk and retrieved a folded piece of paper. He kept his eyes on Chance and handed the paper to Rainey, who opened it and then sank into her chair. She held out the paper to Danny. He looked at an image of the people Rainey loved most in the world, taken at the soccer game a few hours earlier. She didn't see Danny's face blanch and then flush red, but she knew him well enough to know that it had.

He shouted, "Lieutenant Holmes, we need you in here."

Holmes burst into the room.

Danny pointed at Chance. "I want full restraints on this inmate, now."

Without hesitation, Holmes pressed the talk button on his radio, "Unit One to Quad 4. I need full restraints at my location." Chance did not resist, as Holmes stepped around the desk. "On your feet inmate."

Chance stood and placed his hands behind his back, a move he completed from the muscle memory of eight years of penitentiary routine. He focused on Rainey. "Someone doesn't want me to talk to you. That's your family in that picture, isn't it? Did you read the warning in the text of the email?"

Rainey snatched the paper from Danny's hand and read aloud the words printed above the image.

"One came with questions. She can't ask anymore. You were warned. Who will be the first to go? Eeny, meeny, miny, moe."

#

"Hello, this is Mommy's phone. Who are you?"

"Weather?"

"Nee Nee!"

"Are you supposed to have Mommy's phone?"

"Mommy's not here, so I ans—"

A rustling noise interrupted Weather's answer.

Rainey asked, "Aren't you supposed to be at Gran's?"

"Oh, hi, Rainey. Yes, the kids are still at my house," Katie's mother said.

"I'm sure there is some purely innocent reason for Weather having Katie's phone."

"According to my granddaughter, it accidentally ended up in her tiny little purse. The purse I nearly had to cut the zipper out of to retrieve the phone. Katie is coming to pick it up while they are out and about."

"So, you've talked to Katie?"

"Yes, about an hour ago. She called from home, just before she and Cathleen headed out. She said she left a message on your phone."

"I'm not allowed to have my cell phone inside the prison."

"Rainey, is everything all right?"

"Everything is fine, Melanie. I just need to talk to Katie. Have her call me back at—hang on." She looked at the CO behind the desk. "Does this direct line show up on caller I.D.?" The CO nodded. "Melanie, tell her to call the number on the caller I.D. They will know how to find me."

"I'll tell her."

Rainey hesitated before she said, "Keep the kids close today, okay?"

"I will." Melanie's apprehensive sigh reminded Rainey that Katie's mother had also lived through the threats to their lives. She must have realized her uneasiness had been audible and quickly added, "Stay safe."

"Always."

Rainey handed the phone receiver to the CO at the desk, before turning to Danny. "Weather has Katie's phone again. Would you try reaching Cathleen?"

"I did. It went straight to voice mail. Her phone must still be in the bag of rice. I took a shot anyway. You have OnStar. Did you try calling the van?"

"I'd have to go get my phone out of the car. I have the number stored in it." Rainey turned toward the first exit door she saw. "Come on, we have to go."

Danny grabbed her arm. "Rainey, stop. Our only hope of finding out who Chance is working with is to stay here and question him."

"So you think he's playing puppet master," Rainey replied.

"Yes. Somebody on the outside has to be helping him."

"But Katie doesn't know she could be in trouble or the kids. She doesn't know—"

"Katie knows, Rainey. She knows she's always in trouble. You have taught her well. She isn't alone. It is Cathleen's nature to be observant and cautious. She's smart and not without skills. She's a trained soldier, a former Captain in the Army. Those two can handle themselves for a few hours, while we get to the bottom of this, and he can't contact anyone if we don't leave him alone." He paused to make Rainey give him eye contact, before concluding with, "Put your fear aside for the moment. Don't let him see your weakness."

Rainey asked, "And what is my weakness, SSA McNally?"

"You love your family."

"Don't you think he might want me here to leave my family vulnerable?"

Danny seemed to think it through. His eyes never leaving Rainey's, she watched him assess the situation. They were a good team. Their differing approaches and dispositions meant they covered more ground. She let him pause without disturbing his process.

When he finally spoke, his words were calm and measured. "You know this case. You know this man. Is he a serial murderer? I've read your notes. You always added the caveat, 'or he knows something.' You have suspected other family, or Hale Trucking employees were involved in these cases. If that's true, which is more productive; questioning a known participant as opposed to hunting an unknown subject?"

Rainey looked out the window at the end of the hallway. Thunder rumbled as the predicted storm rolled in. Raindrops spotted the panes of glass. Cement mullions served as barriers to escape. Trapped, that about summed up Rainey's situation. Stay inside with Chance Hale or go running around looking for a threat without a clue where it could come from—those were her options.

The gentle rain became a loud roaring squall, as the clouds opened up outside. The clap of thunder and flash of quickening lightning in the raging spring storm joined the beeps and blips of hospital noises. The lights flickered, sending staff scrambling to silence startled alarms. Another roll of thunder shook the building.

Rainey began walking back to the room where they left Chance Hale in shackles. "Come on, Danny. Mother Nature is playing my dramatic entrance music."

As he hurried to land in step with her, Rainey couldn't help the smile when she heard him say, "Cloud up and rain on his ass, Rainey Bell." He chuckled. "I forgot how much I missed saying that."

14

"Why would you involve me in your life again, Chance?" Rainey asked. "You have been off my radar for years."

"You really don't know, do you?"

"Enlighten me," Rainey challenged.

She had started her question before her hand left the door handle. She went about moving the furniture as Chance answered. Danny didn't need instruction. He saw immediately what she was doing and joined in. Chance, now in ankle and waist chains, looked on curiously.

He answered Rainey's question, "There is a new prosecutor in Florida. He came to see me. Said he was considering charging me with murdering Cindy Joan Amen. He based his theory on the evidence located in my truck in 2009 and assumptions found in written notes you left with the detective on the case. I've read them. You jumped to a lot of conclusions."

"Those notes associated you with at least eleven bodies, Chance."

"The prospects of my defense accusing you of planting all that evidence swayed the D.A. not to charge me back them." Chance could not hide his smile, though he covered it with a compliment. "You did a fine linkage-investigation of a killer, former Agent Bell, but it wasn't me. I'm hoping you can help me figure out who it is."

At this point, Danny and Rainey had moved the desk out of the way and pulled the three chairs close together. "Breath stealing distance," her dad would have called it. Rainey called it removing barriers to complete control of her suspect. The only way to make a man who is used to confinement feel more uncomfortable is to make his space even smaller. When she and Danny sat down, they were nearly touching Chance's knees with their own.

"Well, then. We can help each other," Rainey said. "You're going to help me find out who took that picture and emailed it to you."

"It's the same person that murdered all those girls," Chance reiterated.

"Good, then we have a common cause. You apparently have been thinking about this for years. Who do you believe it is?"

Chance broke into a broad smile. "So, you're going to help me?"

Rainey noted that this was not duping delight. It was a genuine display of glee at the prospects of her re-involvement in his case. Either Chance's plan was to get close to her for whatever reason, or he was innocent and believed she could help. A psychopath could mimic an honest man when cornered, Rainey reminded herself.

"I'll ask again. What's your theory?"

Chance scooted to the edge of his seat, bumping knees with Rainey in the process. His cuffed wrists attached to a ring on a belt-chain around his waist limited his movement. He pointed toward the boxes in the corner.

"Blackman sent this stuff over when he stopped being my lawyer. You're going to need the information in the white box on top. The bottom box is my vehicular manslaughter case, which won't interest you."

"Blackman stopped cleaning up your messes. Why is that?" Rainey asked.

"I used up my shares of Hale Trucking, borrowing money against it. Blackman was retired. He had already worked a deal for me to be out in eight to ten on a fifteen-year sentence. I waved appeals to get that chunk lopped off. I didn't need a lawyer until now. Know any good ones?"

Chance chuckled. Rainey and Danny did not.

Chance continued, "Blackman sent all my files to the trucking office. After I had sobered up in prison, I asked to have them brought here so I could study them."

"What's in the files?" Rainey asked while Danny moved the top box to the desk they had pushed up against the wall.

Rainey followed Danny and helped unpack obsessively neat, clearly labeled file folders from one of the boxes, as Chance answered her question.

"With what Blackman sent and what is available as public record, I compiled these files on the murders you connected with me."

Rainey corrected him. "You connected yourself. All I had to do was follow your trail."

Chance ignored her comment. "There were a few surprises in your report."

"Like what?"

"You were looking at me for those early murders, the ones that happened before I met you." Chance paused, for his smile to be seen, before saying, "And the fact that you stalked me up and down the east coast. I was on your mind a lot for many years. That's an odd thing to know about a person—that they've been thinking of you."

Danny interrupted Chance's rumination. "You have copies of actual evidence in here. How did you come to possess this material?"

The question shifted Chance's focus from Rainey.

"Blackman asked his D.A. friend for a copy of all the evidence found in my toolbox. He said he wanted to prepare for the inevitable charges the feds were determined to have filed against me." He pointed at Rainey. "I think he meant her."

Rainey ignored the jab and instead noted for Danny, "There is a folder for each I-95 corridor victim, the ones that showed up at Quantico addressed to me."

"That's a real conundrum, isn't it? If I were the killer, why would I deliver to the police and eventually the FBI the bones of women who trace back to me? Yet, if I'm the guy you think I am, I would definitely taunt you with my ability to hide in plain sight."

Rainey quipped, "Or you're just a psychopath who felt ignored." She grabbed a handful of files. "Are these files color-coded?"

Chance attempted to stand and then thought better of it when his movement drew Danny's attention.

He asked politely, "May I step over to the desk?"

Danny helped Chance stand and stayed close to him as he shuffled up next to Rainey.

"There are thirteen folders, one for each murder or assault victim law enforcement tried to tie to me," Chance explained. "The blue folders are I-95 corridor victims. The plain manila folders are for victims along the route traveled by Hale Trucking vehicles from Hillsborough, North Carolina to Pembina, North Dakota."

Danny held up two red folders. "What about these?"

"That's Gaskill and Travis, two sexual assaults I was questioned about."

Rainey picked up the lone green folder. She opened it to see articles about Alyson Grayson. Chance had kept a close eye on the case. The file contained articles written on the five, ten, and fifteen-year anniversaries of her disappearance.

Chance looked over Rainey's shoulder and commented, "She was a really nice person. I liked her, but I was awkward and drunk or high most of the time."

"She should have gone home that night and left your ass to freeze," Rainey said while staring at a picture of Alyson from a Pembina Weekly News article.

"But then you and I may have never met," Chance said.

Rainey wanted to react with the anger she felt at his cavalier attitude toward Alyson. Instead, she closed the folder without comment. She needed Chance to be cooperative. He needed to make a mistake. He had eight years to strategize for this moment. Rainey had to let him run his script until the opportunity arose to disrupt his plan.

"You share your father's penchant for organized documentation," Danny said.

"You do know Joshua Hale isn't my father. He is actually a half-brother. OB, my grandfather-slash-biological father, was a warped old man surrounded by even more disturbed women, made so by his tyrannical abuse."

Rainey noted, "I understand most people who knew him thought OB stood for Old Bastard."

"That's what he was," Chance said. "He was mean as that lion he kept. Her name was Geordie. She hated everybody but ol' Obadiah. It wasn't affection that tamed her toward him, though. She was scared of him, just like the rest of us. OB had her pelt on his bedroom floor and her lower jaw on the mantel. That was OB reminding us that he was in control of how things lived and died."

Danny was incredulous. "He kept a lion?"

"Yes, in the grotto at the back of the property. OB built her enclosure like the one at the zoo he helped build in Oklahoma City during the depression. He ran away from home, ended up on an orphan train, ran away again, then lied about his age to work with the CCC. OB never lived a normal life, not even as a kid.

"Did you know OB worked the circus too, when he was young and after the war? He liked to tell how he bought his first truck with money he made before he was twelve. More than likely he stole the truck just like that bullhook he always carried. OB told people he took it off the man that tried to beat him with it when he was fourteen-years-old, an old bull man he said. That's the guy that works the elephants in the circus."

Danny chuckled and said, "This shit keeps getting weirder and weirder. What happened to the lion?"

Chance let out a short but deliberate sigh, before his tale began.

"One of the few memories I have of my mother involves that lion. She tried to befriend Geordie. She would haul me out to the grotto after supper when I was just a toddler. We would give Geordie scraps saved from clearing the dishes. I was four years old when OB cornered her on the cage side of the grotto. She pushed him away. He backhanded her so hard that I clearly remember the blood trickling from her nose onto the shoulder of my white tee shirt."

Rainey commented, "That's a lot of violence to witness as a child."

"That's not the worst of it. The old man slipped on the wet concrete and fell against the cage bars. Geordie saw her chance for revenge. She charged and took a swipe at OB, ripped through his shirt, and raked his back with her claws before he could roll away from her. He stood up, nailed Geordie right between the eyes with that bullhook, and then beat her to death in front of us. The message was clear for me fairly early. If you crossed OB, he would kill you."

"Wow, what a fucked up place to grow up," Rainey remarked.

Chance pointed the thumbs of his handcuffed hands at his chest. "And that makes me a perfect candidate for serial murderer. I wet the bed until I was six too. I set fires. I liked to blow things up. I wasn't into torturing animals, but you can pretty much tick off the rest of the boxes you behavioral analysts look for—physical abuse, psychological abuse, a family history of sexual problems and psychiatric issues. I've read the books too."

While he spoke, Chance surveyed the folders on the desk. Rainey had organized them in chronological order, making two purposeful errors in the process. She watched him see the mistakes immediately.

"You've placed Tammy Lynn Gaskill in the wrong place. That happened about a month before the main house blew up in October of 98."

Rainey noted Chance expressed neither penitence nor bereavement when discussing the explosion that killed OB Hale, his wife, Letha, his daughter, Sarah, and his son-in-law, Roger Hughes. Chance should have been in the house. The fact that he was elsewhere on the property was suspicious. Having a police officer show up to his exact location and then swear Chance was passed-out drunk when the house exploded was almost too convenient.

Instead of showing concern for dead family members, he pointed to a manila folder, reaching out as far as his waist chains would let him, but not far enough. "Sharon Long should come after the Abrahamsen file."

Rainey disregarded his need for her to correctly display the files. His OCD necessity for order left him vulnerable.

She feigned a lack of knowledge. "What happened with that explosion? Killed a bunch of family members, didn't it?"

"Gee said—"

96

"Wait, are you talking about Jean Berry?" Rainey asked, remembering the redhead she met in Pembina.

"No, she's Jean. Eugene is her son. We just called him Gee."

Rainey asked, "Does Jean Berry come visit you?"

"Yes, she writes to me sometimes, or she used to. But she never comes to the prison. Gee came a couple of times."

Danny redirected the conversation. "What did Gee say happened the night the house exploded?"

"He said OB got mad about something and drove off in a huff earlier in the day, but not before he backed the pickup into the propane tank behind the house. Gee and Roger looked at the damage but didn't see the pipefitting knocked loose in the basement. It leaked gas for hours. It was a cold night. The heater kicked on, and that was all she wrote. I am lucky I wasn't blamed for that too."

"You are luckier that you weren't home in bed like the others, wouldn't you say?"

Rainey asked the question while placing the Sharon Long folder in the correct spot in the order. Chance showed some relief, but he could not let go of the Gaskill file's improper placement. He stared at the folder, not acknowledging the question. Rainey placed her fingertip on the folder and appeared prepared to move it, but stopped to ask Danny a question.

"SSA McNally, do you think we could get a copy of the report on that explosion? I'd like to see the investigators' findings."

Danny knew what she was doing. If he didn't, one look at Chance would have given it away. He was breaking a sweat. His breathing became shallower. He was stressing out over one folder out of place.

Danny extended the torture. "Lieutenant Holmes said he'd bring a phone in here so I can hook up with Quantico. Brooks can find anything we don't have here."

Chance still stared at the Gaskill folder. He was almost there. Rainey tried to push him over the edge. Her finger played with the folder, moving it only slightly.

She dragged out the pain for Chance, telling Danny, "Hey, see if we can get some water. Coffee might be pushing it, but if they offer, I'll take mine black."

Danny asked, "When did you stop using cream and sugar? It was always two and two for you."

"How sweet that you remember how I liked my coffee, but Katie made me drop sugar and dairy."

"But you just ate a cheeseburger on the way up here."

Rainey laughed. "Shh, don't tell on me."

Very quietly and trying desperately not to show his anxiousness, Chance said, "The Gaskill folder goes after the Alyson Grayson file."

Danny pretended not to hear. "Cathleen is after me to eat healthier too."

"Although I cheat occasionally, I do feel better. You should try it," Rainey said, just before Chance lost it.

Through a clenched jaw, he said, "I know what you're doing. You didn't come here unprepared. You know my OCD is an issue. Please, put the folders in order or mess them up, but don't leave just that one out of place."

Rainey took the Gaskill folder out of the line of files on the desk.

"Is that better?" She asked with a knowing smile.

Chance sighed with relief. "I can't help how my disorder makes me feel. It got worse after I got off the drugs and alcohol. Rationally, I understand it, but it doesn't help me cope. The COs tease me about my cell. They will toss it just to watch me scramble to put it all back in place. Those steroid junkies are the worst, just waiting for a reaction so they can pound an inmate."

Rainey gave no credence to Chance's plea for pity. She picked up the Gaskill file and noted the worn edges. A quick glance down the line at the other well-handled folders told Rainey the one she held had garnered a lot of extra attention.

"You've spent some time with these folders."

Of course, Chance had spent hours with his files, pouring over each detail. Innocent or guilty, these files were an obsession. As the rust bucket to showpiece truck restoration exemplified, Chance's preoccupation with detail was a defining element of his personality.

Rainey dug a bit deeper into the family tragedy. "Before we get to the files, I want to ask you about the people that died that night in the explosion. You hated OB. You've made that clear. What about your grandmother, Letha? She helped raise you. Was she one of OB's 'disturbed' women, as you called them?"

"Yes, I'd say she was. Letha was simple and beaten down, like a trapped animal. She was happy to cook, sew, and work in her garden. I don't remember Letha ever leaving the home place unless she was too sick to wait on OB. He'd send her to the hospital and fetch her when they had pumped the life back into her. When I was young, I couldn't figure out why she came back. Why didn't she run? I get it now. She was a prisoner in OB's home, both physically and mentally. Free will was no longer a concept she understood. I think he may have hit her too hard at some point."

"Did your father, I mean—hell, it's hard to keep this straight. Did Joshua see his father beat his mother?"

"Yes, but OB beat him too, so what was he going to do. Even as a grown man, OB would take the rod end of that ankus to Joshua like he was an animal. He pretty much beat on everybody, so I don't doubt that he clocked Letha a time or two too many."

"So, you felt sorry for her?"

"I was just trying to survive, man. Letha didn't have much to do with me. She favored my cousin Robby. Everyone did."

Danny entered the conversation again. "Let's talk about Robby."

While Danny held his attention, Rainey looked at the Tammy Lynn Gaskill file. The name had not come up in her investigation of Chance Hale. She read the file with one ear tuned to the conversation in the room.

"What about Robby?" Chance asked.

"He's really your half-brother, not a cousin."

"That's correct. His mother is OB's daughter, Sarah."

"And OB is his father," Danny added.

"Yep, that son of a bitch was a piece of work. You'll never hear me say I'm sorry he's dead. I wish he had been killed a lot sooner."

"What about Sarah's husband, Roger? Do you think he knew? Did Robby know?"

"Robby found out when I did back in 2009. We grew up being mistaken for brothers, even after Robby filled out and got taller. We knew our family was weird, but what kid imagines they are the product of incest. OB was in charge, but I say they were all complicit because they hid it so well."

Without looking at him, Rainey could tell by his tone that Danny was not buying the story, when he asked, "What changed in 2009?"

"Rainey is the one that verified what we had suspected. She had that DNA I gave up in 2005 analyzed. She told me about it when I was arrested in 2009. Robby got tested after that. We knew then that we had the same father and it wasn't Joshua. I don't know what Roger knew. He was OB's lackey. He wasn't any better than the women who never stood up to him. They were all stupid enough to let OB treat them like dirt."

Rainey finished reading the file and handed it to Danny, as she replied to Chance's comment.

"Stupid has nothing to do with it. One of the most unexpected facts to emerge in our studies of women involved with sadistic males is how normal these women's lives were before they met him. Most were of average or better intelligence. Many were women one would never expect could be dominated in this way."

Chance tried to hide his smirk but was not successful. He said, "I guess I should read more books written by you profilers. Look, I was just a kid. From what I saw, no one, not one adult ever stood up to that man, not even the cops. How did they expect the children to come out unscathed?"

Rainey told him what she knew to be true. "At some point, they stopped caring. Somewhere in the process, even the most compassionate person can lose their connection to humanity. It often comes down to survival instincts. If they can't save themselves, how in the hell can they save anyone else?"

The door opened, revealing Lieutenant Holmes carrying a phone.

"Here's the phone you requested. You can plug it in over there. Dial zero, identify yourself, and the operator will connect you with an outside line."

Danny said, "Thank you," and took the phone.

Holmes observed the desk with the files spread out and asked, "Is there anything else I can do for you?"

Rainey pointed at Chance's ankle chains. "You can remove those. I don't think Chance is going to make a run for it, but leave the waist chains and cuffs."

"Turn your back to me, inmate," Holmes ordered.

Chance did as he was told and Holmes removed the restraints.

"Anything else? Water? Coffee?"

Danny made up for his earlier bad attitude. "We don't want to be any trouble."

"No trouble at all. I understand a threat has been made to your family." He nodded at Rainey. "Whatever you need, I'll be glad to help."

Rainey responded, "Thank you, very much. Water would be great. We really appreciate your helping us out."

"I'll be right back. If there is anything you need, just ask. I've got kids too."

Holmes left the room. Danny plugged in the phone, dialed zero, and spoke with the operator. Rainey turned back to Chance.

"The body found in the Albemarle Sound, Vanessa Wilhelm. What do you know about her?"

"She wrote a blog about serial killers. She contacted me for an interview about Joshua."

"The man she believed was your father."

"Yes. She was writing a book about the children of serial killers and the permanent stain left on their lives."

"Did you talk to her?"

"At first through letters. Then when I could trust her, we switched to emails. She was waiting to be cleared by the prison for a visit. Then she just disappeared."

"Do you know if Vanessa spoke with anyone else in your family?"

"Well, there's Robby. I understand he is in a long-term care facility after a drug overdose. He was in a coma for a while, and now I'm told he has recovered some function, but suffered permanent brain damage. Gee described him as a toddler with dementia in a man's body. "

"You've always maintained that someone in your family or an employee of Hale Trucking set you up for all these murders. Wasn't Robby your prime suspect?"

"Yes," Chance answered, somewhat defeated, "but it can't be him, not if the person who sent that picture of you is involved. Besides, Robby was already hospitalized by the time Vanessa was killed."

"Why do you think her death is connected to you?"

"Oh, come on. The newspaper said the medical examiner's office believed she died of a head wound and the body was frozen before being placed in the sound. Every woman in these files died of a similar wound and was frozen at some point. That right there should tell you I had nothing to do with those murders."

Rainey reacted to his attempt to clear himself of wrong doing with, "And you could just have easily engaged someone to kill her and make it look like the other murders, as a way to shift suspicion from you before your first parole hearing."

"Like who? Besides my lawyer, before he quit, Gee and his mom are the only people I've communicated with in the eight years I've been in prison. Gee is all bible and forgiveness bull shit. He only comes to try and save my soul. And Jean is kind of in and out of reality, Gee says."

"You talked to Ms. Wilhelm, right? How do we know she's the only serial killer fan you talked to? It wouldn't be the first time some wacko partnered up with a killer on the inside."

"Check my visitor logs. Check the email account I used. The prison records incoming and outgoing mail. They read it too. Look all you want. You'll find nothing there."

Rainey smiled. "There are a number of ways you could have connected with someone on the outside. If you have one email account, you can have more. Don't play dumb, Chance. We know you aren't."

"Rainey," Danny said, to get her attention. "Brooks is on the line."

Melatiah Brooks, part of the Communication and Information Technology Unit, or CITU, and an old friend from her FBI days was an investigative lifeline Rainey knew Danny would miss in his soon to be civilian life. Rainey lost the use of Brooks' skills, but they maintained a close friendship.

Taking the phone receiver from Danny, she said, "Hello, Ms. Brooks."

"Hello, Rainey Bell. I should have known it had been just a little too quiet where you're concerned. Are my babies safe?"

"Safe at Grandma's."

"Where is Katie?"

"She's with Cathleen. They are fine."

"And you?"

"Well, I'm inside a prison, so I think I'm pretty secure."

"All right, then. So, someone is threatening that beautiful family of yours again. I'm already running a search for images and language concerning you all, but it sounds like this was a private email, so I don't expect to find anything."

"I don't expect you will, this time. We need to look at all activity on an email account being used by a prisoner here, illegally I might add," she cut her eyes at Chance, who was watching her closely. "If we can get you access to the computer and the system he used, could you find other accounts he might have but is reluctant to give us."

"Yes. I can compare the known emails with language in the other's and see what pops up."

"Good. I also want to look at an account belonging to a murder victim, Vanessa Wilhelm. Danny will give you the details."

Brooks had a few requests of her own. "I need to speak to the I.T. people there at the prison. It will make this go much faster if I don't have to break through firewalls and security programs."

"Danny can make that happen. Remember, I'm a civilian. People don't jump for me like they do a federal badge."

"With a badge or not, you know I will always jump for you."

"I know, my friend, but let's keep this one above skirting the law levels." Rainey stared straight at Chance. "If we find anything, I don't want it thrown out of court."

"If a prisoner was accessing email illegally, we have legal grounds to see who he's been communicating with. On the Vanessa Wilhelm account, I'm going to need a warrant to access any emails that did not go to the prison."

"Danny can make that happen. She's a murder victim, so a warrant probably already exists for her Internet activity."

"Okay. Tell him to make it happen fast. I'm up to my ample bosom in...well, I'm sure you'll know soon enough. The world will know. What a fucked up mess we have here in DC. That's why I'm in on a Saturday when I should be with my boo watching cherry blossoms bloom."

"You should quit and come work with me," Rainey said. She chuckled, but she was serious.

"If the marmalade man stays in office much longer, I will probably do—"

Rainey heard a man's voice in the background and then Brooks reply, "Yes, sir. I just sent you the email."

Rainey waited for Brooks to return to their conversation. She heard her mumbling, "These fuckers are going to make me lose my mind up in here," before she said, "Okay, Rainey Bell, I've got to go. I'll call you back in about two hours, give or take. Is there anything else, before I go?"

"Yes. There was an explosion on Halloween of '98. The actual date would be November 1st, early morning. It happened at OB Hale's residence, a little south of Hillsborough, North Carolina. That's Orange County's jurisdiction. Four people died. I need the police reports, especially the ones from the State Police and ATF." Rainey eyed Chance again and added to her requests. "Oh, and I need you to find an assault victim, Tammy Lynn Gaskill. She used to live in Orange County, but the assault was recorded in Durham County. She may be married. She'd be about thirty-two years old now. Contact Sergeant Detective Sheila Robertson with the Durham County Sheriff's office. She took the victim's statement."

Chance's eyebrows arched in question.

"Oh, I remember her from your Christmas party last year," Brooks said in Rainey's ear.

"Yes, that's her. Find out if they ever ran the DNA evidence from the Gaskill case through NCIC. The date of the assault was September 25, 1998. If they ran it before 2005, ask her to run it again."

"Will do. Be safe, Rainey Bell."

"Always, my friend. Always."

15

Danny left the room to talk with the prison staff about Chance's access to a computer and to facilitate the I.T. department's communication with Brooks. He also needed a fax machine to work on the warrant for Vanessa Wilhelm's communications with Chance.

Before leaving, he asked, "Will you be all right in here alone? Do you want the Lieutenant to stay with you?"

Rainey looked over at Chance, who had resumed his place in the corner chair.

"No. I don't think we'll have any issues. Right, Chance?"

"Right," he answered, a little more subdued than before.

It was the first time Rainey had ever seen him show a scintilla of guilt concerning an investigation involving him. He had never wavered in his claims of innocence. His reaction to her inquiries into the Gaskill case left a door open. Rainey walked right in. She sat down in the chair across from him and began.

"Okay, Chance. We have been trying to have this conversation since 1998. Let's get this done, once and for all."

Chance, who had been staring at her from under a quizzical brow, blinked back to his mask of innocent cooperation and said, "Okay. Do you want to talk about Alyson first?"

"No. Let's start at the beginning."

"The beginning of what?"

"Your life. What is your first memory?"

Chance thought for a second, before stating, "The day OB killed Geordie. I was four. That's the only memory I have of my mother."

"You said you were four when that happened? That's young for retaining memory."

"I know I was four because she left soon after that. I was never allowed to talk about her ever again. I asked OB about her shortly after she left. He slapped the shit out of me and told me never to mention the 'whore' again. I asked Joshua where she went and he whipped me. I asked Robby, and he punched me in the nose, called my mother a whore, and then told OB all about it. I learned not to ask. You have to understand how discipline worked for OB."

"And how's that?"

"If a family member broke one of OB's rules and another family member knew about it, it had to be dealt with and reported. If Robby hadn't punched me, he would have received a punishment far worse than mine. As it was, I had a bloody nose and a blistered butt, and I never asked about her again. At least not until after they were all dead."

"Who did you ask?"

"I asked Gee about her. He is six years older than me so he could remember her better than I could."

"What did he tell you?"

A cloud of emotion seemed to settle over Chance. He hesitated before answering, "That I shouldn't try to find her. He said my mother tried to kill us."

"Who? Who did she try to kill?"

"Me, Robby, and Gee. Gee was ten. Robby was six. I was four. I don't remember any of it, but he does. He said Naomi—that's my mother's name, Naomi Annalisa—anyway, Gee said she took us out to the grotto for a picnic. She gave us brownies laced with some kind of drug. Gee said he fell asleep and woke up because Robby was screaming. My mother was trying to drown him in the lion's pool. I was already floating face down. He said he pulled me out of the water and ran with me over his shoulder to find Jean. I guess the running knocked the air into me because he remembered I started crying before he found his mom. When they got back, Robby was crying, and my mother was gone."

"Again, wow. That's a horrible thing to live through. Did you and Robby ever talk about it?"

"No. Like I said, OB forbid my mother being mentioned. We couldn't talk about her at all."

"Even when you got older, you never talked about this with Robby?"

"Never. You have to understand; we thought OB was the devil himself. He always seemed to know everything we did and said, like the place was bugged or something."

"What did they say happened to your mother?"

"That the whore ran off with another man. That's what they told anyone that asked. Joshua moved to North Dakota and I was left with OB and Letha."

"Do you really think she ran away?"

"When I was young, I believed it. As I aged, I thought OB or Joshua killed her. I only found out recently that neither of those things happened. My mother was a patient at Central Regional Psychiatric Hospital here in Butner, about a mile and a half from where I'm sitting, from 1987 to 1997."

"How did you find that information?"

"Vanessa Wilhelm. She spent some time digging up info on my family. She found an old neighbor in a nursing home. He told her he found my mother wandering naked on his property and called the police. They took her to the hospital, and he never saw or heard of her again. I sent a request for her records, but they only told me admission and release dates. Vanessa thought my mother must have changed her name because after her release she vanished."

Rainey dug further. "What about her mother? We know OB was her father. Who was her mother? Do you know?"

"Since I was forbidden to talk about Naomi, I never asked where she came from, but I have wondered who her mother was. She's probably dead, because I would have seen her around, don't you think? It had to be someone OB controlled and he never let anyone go once he had them. Did you know my mother was just twelve years old when I was born, thirteen when she married Joshua? She disappeared. Why couldn't her mother have disappeared the same way?"

"It's no wonder your mother needed psychiatric care. It appears you all did, except for Gee. He hasn't been in any trouble with the law, has he?"

"Not that I'm aware of," Chance answered.

"Is he OB's son too?"

"Well, I guess he could be. Jean Berry wasn't just his office manager. But, Gee doesn't look like the rest of us. We're all blond-haired and blue-eyed. Gee has his mother's red hair, and his eyes are hazel. OB wouldn't beat on Gee like he did us, either. Jean wouldn't allow it."

"Jean stood up to OB?"

"Yeah, over Gee anyway. Maybe it's because he was born with a clef pallet and was kind of sickly. Gee didn't talk well or much and had lots of operations when he was a kid. He stayed quiet, even after they fixed him up. There was just that little scar on his lip, but I think the internal scars took a lot longer to heal. He's okay now. You only hear the lisp really well when he's excited. He had a mustache and beard the last time I saw him. You can't even see the scar. He turned out to be the best of us all. That's why I don't think he's kin to us. He's too good."

Rainey shook her head. "Wow. That's one messed up family you got there, Chance."

"You have no idea how fucked up that old man was. Once, when I was nine or ten, Robby and I found a trunk Joshua had stored up in the loft of the big truck garage. It was full of old sadistic bondage magazines. Some had Nazi women torturing men on the covers. Others were a lot worse, with pictures of women being tortured in every way imaginable. It was horrible. I can still remember those pictures clearly. Robby thought it was cool. He even got a boner looking at that shit."

"And you didn't?"

Chance hesitated before he answered. "Well, I mean there were naked women. So yeah, I got a little excited, but Robby was really into it."

He apparently wanted to move away from the topic of his own arousal and quickly began to describe what happened next.

"Anyway, while we were up in the loft, the door opened downstairs and in walks OB and one of the drivers. OB leased his trucks to drivers and took a percentage of profit from each load. This particular driver had shorted OB on a load payment. OB took his truck. He came that day with his wife to ask forgiveness and to get his truck back. I guess he thought OB wouldn't beat his ass if he had his wife there. Bad move."

"Did he beat him in front of her?"

"No, worse. OB told the guy he could have the truck back, but the wife had to work off the debt. The guy was in his twenties I think, and his wife was young and beautiful. OB laid her across the hood of a car in the garage and raped her right in front of her husband. When the guy changed his mind and tried to stop him, OB cracked him on the head with his ankus and finished what he started. When he was done, he handed the woman the keys to the truck and walked out, like it was just another day at the office."

"Did you and Robby tell anyone what you saw?"

"No. I told you it was OB's rules that mattered, not morality. Besides, I freaked out because when I turned around Robby was jacking off. He got off on that, just like the magazines. That's why I always thought Robby was the one killing those women. In fact, I was sure it was him. I know he knew one of those girls they found in the pond in North Dakota."

Rainey stood and walked to the desk where the files were. "Which one?"

"Adeline Tuttle. When I saw her picture in the news articles after she was found, I knew I had seen her with Robby."

Rainey picked up the four manila file folders and came back to sit with Chance.

She asked him, "Why didn't you tell anyone what you knew, instead of letting people think it was you?"

"Robby always got away with everything. I thought if I told what I knew, I'd end up being blamed anyway. Plus, Robby was the only family member that treated me decent. I was fourteen and not exactly thinking clearly."

"Does any fourteen-year-old think clearly?"

Rainey took note of the growing tension in Chance's jaw muscles as he continued his tale of growing up in the Hale household.

"Growing up in that environment, I was really messed up. I was already an alcoholic by thirteen. I smoked a lot of pot. I took any kind of drug I could find without a thought of what it could do. I didn't care about living or dying. I just went numb, kept my head down, and buried the pain deep. The only time I was sober was when I worked on the trucks. OB had me in the shop with him almost all the time. After sixth grade, I didn't really go to school much—just enough to keep the law off OB for not sending me."

Rainey steered the conversation back to the files in her hand. "Let's get back to Adeline Tuttle. Where did you see Robby with her?"

"In the supply truck, we used to haul gear to North Dakota. We stopped in Greensboro to get some food. She had the hood up on her car, and Robby asked if he could help her."

"Was Robby a mechanic too?"

"No way. Robby wouldn't know a head gasket from a spark plug. He drove trucks. He didn't work on them."

Rainey knew the case history from memory. She didn't have to refer to the file for the details, but she checked to see if Chance's files held what she already knew. After a quick review of the file's contents, she continued.

"Are you using the information in this file to conjure a story that conveniently blames a man that can't defend himself?"

Chance sighed. "I'm never going to win with you."

"Come on, Chance. You have to see this through my eyes. Witnesses said they saw a young man with long blond hair leaning under Adeline's car hood and talking to her in the parking lot of the restaurant. You are blond. You are the mechanic. Wouldn't it be more plausible that it was you they saw?"

"Yes, it would, if several witnesses hadn't also commented on the other blond young man throwing up behind the truck. That was me. I had a stomach virus, but I went with Robby on the supply run just to get away from home. After I got sick, I crawled back in the truck and went to sleep. When I woke up, Robby was pulling back on the highway. I didn't think anything of it until I saw her picture in the paper."

Rainey sat back against the chair. She had almost been lulled into pity for Chance, but then he let a self-satisfied expression flicker on and then retreat from his face. He was good at hiding his true nature. She had to give him that. Rainey's upper lip curled into a sneer before she hid it in a slight smile. She saw him see it. His duping delight flashed in a brief grin, but long enough for Rainey to see this psychopathic tell. Chance was right about being able to check off the serial killer survey boxes with him, including his convenient way of explaining away all the clues that pointed to him.

"Chance, as far as I can tell, you have an excuse for everything. Poor little boy. His mommy left him. His daddy, well, I mean that's just a total fucking mess. Somehow you had the dumb luck to be brought into the world by a family of killers and rapists. Is that it? Look at you, all educated now, clean and sober. No way you're guilty of anything other than the crime for which you've done your time. You're just an innocent soul who, despite your name, never had a chance. Is that what you want me to think?"

Danny walked through the door at that exact moment. Rainey heard him, but she did not lose focus on Chance. Her flat response caused Chance's expression to melt into the cold gaze she encountered on the floor of that kitchen all those years ago, before he quickly resumed his innocuous visage.

Rainey's father, Billy Bell, gave her much instruction on reading people and their intentions. The piece of advice she had used the most in her law enforcement career involved what he called "the check." Billy chased bail jumpers. He made life-saving decisions in the blink of an eye.

"They pluck the strings of a sad ballad, sing you a tune of woe and misery," Billy would say, "and some of it might even be true. Hell, it could all be true, but what motivates the telling is more important than the story. And if the perp is checking to see if he's believable, my instinct says whatever truth he is telling is covering up a lie."

Rainey knew she was right about Chance. Now, she had to prove it.

"Is everything okay in here?" Danny asked.

Rainey turned to him and saw he was holding a file folder in one hand.

She answered his question, "Yep, just peachy," and then asked, "Did you get Brooks all set up?"

"She's hooked into the facility's system. I spoke with Detective Robertson myself. She headed into her office to pull the Gaskill file and

109

send the DNA report to our lab. The Orange County Sherriff's Department is emailing the files on the Hale house explosion to your business address." He shifted his eyes to Chance. "And fortunately the State Bureau of Investigation already has a warrant for Wilhelm's web activity. Their investigator is in touch with Brooks. If there is anything, anything at all, she will find it."

Rainey joined Danny in glaring at Chance. "Good. We'll know soon enough where that picture came from. Since the Gaskill case DNA has already been processed, the comparison is just a matter of entering the data. Technology is a beautiful thing."

She paused just long enough to notice the change in prominence of Chance's temple vein, as it throbbed against his skin.

"Now, where were we? Oh yeah, Chance here was giving up his cousin-slash-half-brother in connection with one of the frozen pond victims in North Dakota, complete with a convenient excuse for his not being involved."

Rainey held out the Tuttle file to Danny as he moved to sit in the chair next to her. He exchanged the folder he carried for the one Rainey was holding out to him and began to speak, giving her time to look inside what appeared to be an empty file. She found a single page of copy paper with a hand-written note.

"Katie fine. Has her phone now. Going out to an early dinner and a movie with Ann and Cathleen. She is aware of the threat and at DEFCON 4. Will be home around 9 pm."

Under the neatly printed information, Danny had written in larger print within quotation marks, "Don't overreact." Beneath the quote, he had written, "Her words," and underlined it three times. At the bottom of the page, Danny had written, "I have interesting notes from Sheila."

Rainey didn't have much time to wonder why Danny hadn't come to get her to speak with Katie personally. Knowing her wife, how he delivered the message probably was not Danny's choice. Katie did not believe in worrying about things before she really needed to be concerned. With the "aware of the threat" line, Katie had acknowledged an increased intelligence watch and strengthened security measures. After six years of risk assessment and actual near death experiences, Katie had developed her own way of dealing with being Rainey Bell's wife.

Rainey looked up when she heard Danny ask Chance, "How old were you in June of 1996, fourteen?"

"Yes. That is correct."

Rainey noted Chance had regained his polite and cooperative demeanor.

Danny gave the Tuttle file back to Rainey and pulled his notepad from the inside breast pocket of his suit jacket. He flipped it open and asked, "You went to live in North Dakota when you were fourteen, didn't you?"

"Yes. I started school there in the Fall of 1996."

"And why was that?"

Chance stalled. "I'm sorry. What are you asking?"

"Why did you leave North Carolina? If OB was as controlling as you've said, why did he let you go?"

One of the first things drilled into BAU agents was to never ask a question without knowing the actual answer. Rainey was anxious to know what that answer could be, but first, they had to hear Chance's version.

"They needed a mechanic on call at the north garage pretty much twenty-four hours a day. I was really cheap labor. They paid me just enough to keep a full supply of Canadian weed and booze on hand. Joshua was on the road most of the time. An unsupervised fourteen-year-old, what could go wrong?"

Chance chuckled at his witty comment, while his eyes searched the faces of his interrogators for clues they believed his version of events.

Danny obviously did not. He pressed on. "Adeline Tuttle disappeared on Friday, June 7, 1996. You were questioned on Thursday, June 6th, in the sexual assault of a thirteen-year-old female on the previous Saturday, June 1st. Care to talk about that?"

Chance reacted with surprise. "Wow. You guys are good. I was never charged with that assault and, as far as I know, the girl said she was too drunk to remember which one of a dozen boys at that party assaulted her. I learned later that she and her parents moved away. End of story."

"So, OB didn't pay the family to go away. Are you saying that part of what I'm being told isn't true?"

Chance was interested now. He leaned forward slightly, trying to sneak a glimpse at Danny's notes. Unsuccessful in the attempt, he answered, "Not to my knowledge. There was no reason to pay them off. She was wasted and got in over her head with some older boys. She couldn't remember what happened."

Rainey drew Chance's attention with her question. "You sound as if you know what happened."

"I just know what Robby told me. I was wasted and passed out in the back of his truck. He said some of the guys had sex with her and she was more than willing. I'm not making any judgments. That's just what he said."

Danny read from his notepad, "Emily Dawson. Her name was Emily Dawson." He glared at Chance long enough to make it clear how he felt about his arrogant attitude. "Emily tested positive for sedatives and near-lethal blood alcohol concentration levels after her parents found her the next morning in their backyard. She required stitches to repair tearing." He glared at Chance again. "Do you think that sounds consensual?"

Chance first defended himself, "Hey, it wasn't me," and then seemed to realize he needed to show empathy. "Of course it wasn't consensual. I'm sorry that happened to her." He was doing well, mimicking concern, but just had to add, "But I didn't really know her."

Rainey flipped open another file out of the stack she held on her lap. She began a series of rapid-fire questions.

"Did you go back to North Carolina for Christmas in 1996? It would have been your first holiday after moving to live with Joshua."

"Yes. Robby drove the supply truck up, and I caught a ride down to pick up that '51 Chevy I was restoring. Joshua came down, and we hauled it back to North Dakota on a flatbed trailer behind his rig."

"I don't suppose you remember the dates you were traveling," Rainey said with a smirk.

"No, but I know the dates you are interested in."

"And those would be?"

"On Saturday, December 21, 1996, Madison Parker, age fifteen, disappeared from Burke, Wisconsin and was found in Sinclair Lewis Park in Minnesota thirteen days later."

Chance rattled off the specifics from memory, proving his obsession with the files and the information they contained. He also could not resist giving himself an out.

"I can tell you that the window of opportunity was there for at least three of OB Hale's sons to have abducted and murdered Madison. This is also true for Sharon Long, age sixteen, who went missing from the same Sinclair Lewis Park on July 3, 1997. We met up in Carolina for the Fourth of July."

"You left one out," Rainey said, "The one found in the pond with Adeline Tuttle."

"Ah, yes, Inge Ruth Abrahamsen, age sixteen, disappeared from Minneapolis, March 14, 1997. I looked it up. I was out of school for a break, not that it mattered much. I barely went. I did go back and forth on the supply truck with Robby quite often. I can't say for sure if it was that weekend or not."

"Did the supply truck run the route frequently?"

"Yeah, pretty much once a week. Robby started running parts as soon he turned sixteen. When you have refrigerated trucks and freezer rigs, there is always something to fix."

Danny couldn't believe how tightly this case fit Chance Hale. He asked, "Your family ran a fleet of refrigerator rigs?"

"Yeah, we hauled frozen goods as a specialty. OB's motto was 'Ride cold as Hale.' He had it painted on the back doors of our rigs."

112

Danny shook his head and chuckled. He turned to Rainey and said, "You were right. This guy is either the most unlucky man in the world, or he's a serial murderer born into the perfect storm."

"It's all circumstantial," Chance cried out. Frustrated, he slapped his hands on his thighs.

Rainey recited, "Circumstantial evidence relies on logic to reach an assumption of fact—like a fingerprint at the scene of a crime that can be explained away easily. But the same fingerprint at five similar crime scenes can logically lead to an assumption of linkage."

Chance shot back, "Like I said, you've made a lot of assumptions, and you don't have a single fingerprint. There is nothing in this room that connects me directly to any of these crimes."

Rainey saw Chance pause briefly, as he looked around the room to emphasize her lack of evidence. She followed his eyes and could not believe she had not seen it sooner. It was time to end Chance's charade of innocence.

"I don't have a fingerprint, but what I do have is—"

Rainey held up the folders one at a time and continued.

"Eileen Baker, last seen with you in Portland, Maine on January 29, 1999. Her partial remains left in St. Augustine, Florida on January 30, 2000, before ending up at the FBI lab with my name on them. You were in St. Augustine in the winter of 2000."

Rainey slapped that folder down on the desk and held up another.

"Cindy Joan Amen, last seen with a man fitting your description in St. Augustine, Florida on February 6, 2000. Her remains turned up in Savannah, Georgia in August of 2001—with another request to forward the box to me at Quantico. You were in Charleston, South Carolina that fall."

She slapped the Amen folder down on the desk.

"Kristen Maria Patton, last seen in Charleston on August 3, 2001, with you. Her remains were left with the police in Wilmington, Delaware in May of 2002 and forwarded to me at Quantico."

Down went the Patton folder.

"Rebekah Nell Hagen, last seen on May 20, 2002, on the boardwalk at Rehoboth Beach, Delaware. She was walking with a tall young man with long blond hair. Her remains showed up in Gloucester, Massachusetts in April of 2003, again forwarded to me. You were working in Gloucester at the time."

Slap.

"Jill Frances Wheaton went missing from Gloucester in April of 2003. Her remains appeared when you did in Newburyport, Massachusetts, in May of 2004. Her remains are also at the FBI lab."

Slap.

"Margaret Mary Hedrick, last seen in Newburyport in May of 2004. Her remains arrived in Norfolk, Virginia in June of 2005 and landed in Quantico just days before you were questioned in the assault on Donna Hollis Travis in Newport News, Virginia."

Slap. Rainey held up her empty hands.

"There are no more folders because you left the United States and did not return until January of 2009. The cases they questioned you about in South America would probably read the same. If you did not commit these crimes, you know the person that did. Nothing has changed in this narrative since the prison doors closed behind you, Chance. I have no reason to change my mind about you either."

Rainey crossed the room to the box left sitting in the corner. The one Chance said they did not need to see. The one his eyes paused on a few minutes before.

"Like you said, it is circumstantial evidence at best, which I'm sure is the reason you have never been brought to trial. But like all criminals, you have made a mistake somewhere, and it will bite you square in the ass in the end."

Chance crossed his arms and leaned back against his chair. He did not attempt to hide his self-satisfied smile, but it slipped when Rainey reached down and tore one of the flaps off the top of the remaining box in the corner.

She faced him, waving the piece of cardboard in the air. "You know, I knew I'd seen this type of box before."

Chance, still smug, said, "It's just a box. What of it?"

Rainey wore the smug smile now. "It's hardly just a box. It's physical evidence."

Chance uncrossed his arms and leaned forward. "What? Evidence of what?"

"Where did this box come from?"

"Blackman sent the files to the trucking office, and Gee brought it to me. I told you that."

Rainey pointed at the box by the desk, the one from which the files had been removed. "That is a Blackman Law Firm box. Look on the end. You can see his filing system numbers."

"How would you know?" Chance asked.

"Just take my word that I can prove what I'm saying."

"Why should I take your word. You've been trying to put me in prison for murders I did not commit since I was sixteen."

Rainey leaned down, putting her face inches from Chance's nose. "That's right. I know you. I know who you are. I've seen through the different faces you wear to where the evil you were born into hides and waits. I know you couldn't help but put evidence under my nose just so you could relish in your self-perceived superiority. Just like you couldn't resist sending those bones to Quantico, to me personally, in a box just like that one there."

Chance glared at Rainey. Through gritted teeth, he said, "You're bullshitting. You can't match boxes. That company must have made millions of those."

Rainey did not try to hide the sneer that curled her lip. "I guess you didn't know the manufacturer can identify the batch from the fiber composition. What do you think the chances are that the boxes sent to Quantico and this one could have come from the same batch? Do you think we could get a jury to make the logical assumption of linking those boxes to you?"

It was plain from Chance's expression he was afraid that was exactly what was going to happen. Danny, who had been quietly watching the exchange, stood and began walking toward the door.

On his way by, he took the cardboard flap from Rainey's hand and said to Chance, "We're in a cancer ward. I'm sure there is a lab around here that can take a microscopic picture of the fibers in this box. A comparison with the boxes they have at Quantico should take a few hours, but we'll know soon enough."

Chance glowered at Rainey, who was still inches from his nose.

"Will it be fast enough to save your kids from the person who set me up and is now trying to bury me in this hell hole?"

Rainey backed away from Chance. Not because he frightened her, but because she thought she might punch him if she stayed where she was.

Calming her rage, she said, "I have no doubt you have a partner. It's time to pay him a visit."

Rainey reached for the phone plug in the wall. Chance flinched. Rainey chuckled. She unplugged the phone from the wall and removed the cord.

"Don't want you making any phone calls while no one is looking," she said to Chance.

"Do we have everything we need from here?" Danny asked as he waited at the doorway.

Rainey stood over Chance. "Let's make sure this asshole can't talk to anybody, I mean no one until we have his accomplice in cuffs."

Danny opened the door, which drew Lieutenant Holmes into the room.

"Lieutenant, we need this inmate locked down, completely isolated until you hear from us."

"Consider it done. On your feet inmate."

Danny asked, "Which way to the lab?"

"Down the hall to the right. Take the first left. You can't miss it."

Rainey said, "Hang on a sec."

She walked over to the desk, where she had slapped down the files. One by one, she lifted the folders, opened them, and dumped them onto the desk. When she had emptied them all, she swept them into the box where Chance had once neatly organized and stored them. She then crossed to the corner to retrieve the other box.

"We need to mark this as evidence," she said, as she turned it upside down, letting the contents flutter down on top of Chance's other files."

"Bitch," Chance said, under his breath.

Rainey smiled at him as the Lieutenant jerked his arms from behind.

"You ain't seen nothing yet, Chance O. Hale. You should have let me be. Before, I was just doing my job. Now, it's personal."

Rainey followed Danny from the room. They could hear Chance shouting at them, as they walked toward the lab.

"You're playing right into their hands, Bell. They'll get you and your whole family, just like they got Vanessa."

They could still hear Chance screaming, "I'm innocent," as they turned the corner.

Danny said, "Did you hear that? He said 'they'."

Rainey nodded, responding, "Yep. We're looking for more than one partner."

"Any ideas?" Danny asked as he opened the door to the lab's main office.

"Agent McNally," a voice called out.

Rainey turned to see a CO moving toward them.

"There is a call from a technical analyst at Quantico," the officer said. "She said she could talk to either of you. Oh, and these came for you."

"I'll take it, Danny." She handed him the box. "Go ahead, see what you can do with that sample, and start the chain of custody on this box."

Rainey handed Danny the box and followed the officer back to the nurses' station main desk.

She took the phone receiver offered her and said, "Tell me something good."

PART III

"The self-same moment I could pray;
And from my neck so free
The Albatross fell off, and sank
Like lead into the sea."
— Samuel Taylor Coleridge,
The Rime of the Ancient Mariner

16

Rainey drove her wounded baby, the custom ordered pursuit model Charger SRT8, down through the Piedmont Province of North Carolina. The torrential rains had passed, but the severe storm system moved slowly, pushing quarter to golf ball sized hail and damaging winds out in front of it, toward Hillsborough, where Rainey and Danny needed to be. Dreary, gray, low-hanging clouds filled the atmosphere above. White tendrils of mist the texture of an old man's thinning beard curled down just above the treetops. The gloomy skies above, the new dents on Rainey's car's body, and the ominous clouds directly in their path did not bode well.

"That sky over Durham looks like someone threw a strobe light into a pot of boiling black ink," Rainey said, pointing out the windshield at what lay ahead.

"That's a damn angry sky," Danny said. "Do you want to stop and wait it out?"

"My car is already going to need extensive body work. No need to shy away from storm damage now. Can I tell you I fucking hate Chance Hale?"

Danny chuckled, "You can't seriously think he caused that hail storm?"

"No, but he's the reason my car was not in the garage. He's the reason I am not enjoying a cold beer while watching the NCAA basketball tournament. He's the reason I am looking for a threat to my family on a

Saturday afternoon instead of enjoying the kids being at their grandparents' home for the evening."

"Okay, I concede your deserved indignation," Danny said.

A jagged bolt of horizontal lightning crashed across the sky, followed by an instantaneous thunderclap that vibrated in Rainey's chest.

"Wow," Danny said. "I think maybe we should just pull off and sit for ten minutes and it will be gone.

Rainey slowed to below the speed limit, which she wasn't sure her car would understand.

"I'll try not to catch up to it. We're grounded in the vehicle, and the gust front squall line is way ahead of us. We'll just take this tail wind into Hillsborough."

Brooks had provided information identifying the IP address associated with Jean Berry's network provider as the source of the email sent to Chance. The Hale land and still the home of Jean Berry lay southeast of Hillsborough, below Interstate 40, and only thirty-one minutes from the Butner Federal Correctional Complex on a sunny day.

The leading edge of the storm blew through earlier, littering the highway with small branches and tender new leaves. Drifts of quarter and dimed-sized hail lined the roadway. Thick bolts of lightning shot out of the boiling black ink sky up ahead. It was dangerous. It also stood in the way of Rainey finding the person threatening her family.

Interstate 85 cut southward through rolling hills freshly greened by recent spring rains. Crumbling, ancient stone ridges broke up the undulating horizon. Scattered among the hardwood forest oaks and flowering dogwoods, tall evergreens stood out on the southern slopes. Lakes and rivers snaked through the jigsaw puzzle-worthy scenery. This was the part of the Carolina colony that brought wealthy land developers out of Virginia, where the accent of the antebellum south still tints conversations with implied privilege.

Before leaving Butner, Rainey set up her laptop in its console holder and opened the emails from the various agencies from whom she and Danny had requested information. Orange County sent the arson investigation file. Sheila sent all the info she had on Tammy Gaskill, including the fact that related charges were brought against Robby Hughes for giving a minor a controlled substance and resisting when he was arrested. Because of those charges, Rainey had looked into Jean B. Berry back when that first business card was taken from her father's office. It implicated her but did not prove she sent the card along with the bones to Rainey at Quantico. Yet, the sum of the information Rainey knew about this case suggested that all roads led to Jean Berry.

An alert sounded from Rainey's phone through the hands-free audio system.

"A severe thunderstorm has been detected in the area. Seek shelter and wait for it to pass."

Rainey tightened her grip on the steering wheel. "Well, that's not going to happen."

Danny, who hated storms, tried to ignore the weather as he gathered intelligence on Jean Berry's location, the former home of Hale Trucking.

"I'm looking at the satellite image of the property on Google Earth. The pavement stops at the end of Station Road. Moving forward from there requires going down a gravel path that leads into a thickly wooded area and to Jean Berry's home. In an earlier image taken in winter, most of the leaves are gone. I can see fences and the scar on the ground from the explosion. That is a big hunk of land. This clump of evergreens in the western section must be masking the grotto. I don't see it anywhere else."

"Maybe they tore it down, plowed it under," Rainey suggested.

"There isn't any other scarring evident other than the house explosion site. I gotta tell you, that crater doesn't look like a propane explosion. Didn't the arson investigator suspect OB Hale stored some explosives in his basement? They found traces of plastic explosives in the rubble."

"Who stores contraband C-4 in the family home?" Rainey asked, shaking her head at the absurdity. "And what arson investigator assumes the plastic explosives belonged to the dead man and not the someone who made him dead."

Danny leaned in to get a better look at the image on the computer screen, then said, "Okay, here's a different image and I can clearly see the cage structure over the grotto, as it is described in the police report from the night of the explosion. There are two existing houses, one on either side of the property. The one on the northern boundary is Jean Berry's. There are several large garages on the east end of the property. When this last satellite image was taken, there were still trailers and truck parts scattered about."

Rainey concentrated on the freshly puddled bridge, as they crossed Falls Lake. She asked, "What else do you see? There has to be another way in. Big trucks wouldn't have used Station Road."

Danny manipulated the image. "Yeah, on the north side of the property, parallel to the I-40 service road, there is a wide paved drive that leads to those big garages. You have to take a right there where US 70 splits off and then a left under the interstate to reach it."

Rainey smiled and reminded Danny, "These are the stomping grounds of my misspent youth. I know the Eno River Park area and University like you know Quantico. What I didn't know is that there was still that much undeveloped private land over there."

"The train tracks appear to delineate most of the south side of the property, except where the road runs near the other house location."

"The area is called University Station because that was the train stop for people going to Chapel Hill to the University. They would get off the train at the station and then have to make their way down University Road to the school. There's a creek through the Hale property, Stoney Creek, that connects back up to the Eno River."

The speakers in the car came alive, "You have an incoming call from Katie."

Rainey said, "Don't tell her we're going to question a murder suspect, please," to Danny and then hit the appropriate button on the steering wheel. "Hello, is this the owner of this phone or a tiny imposter?"

"Good, you aren't in prison anymore," Katie's voice filled the car.

"We busted out. I'm glad you have your phone back," Rainey said.

"The kleptomaniac was thoroughly searched for other items she shouldn't have. Why is it always my things she takes off with?"

"She is emulating you. Take the compliment. At least she's over the diamond infatuation. I thought for a while she was a cat burglar in training."

"She's on to communications specialist now. Apparently, the toy phone your mother gave her doesn't do all the things a 'reeEAaal' phone does," Katie whined, imitating their daughter. "I explained that the consequences for touching my phone again would be very real."

"Oh no, not the dreaded consequences," Rainey said, laughing.

Katie chuckled too. "I know, right. She is so your kid. Boundaries are suggestions, not hard rules."

Rainey steered the conversation away from her bad influences on Weather. "How was the movie?"

"We didn't go. We shopped until we were famished and then ate until we couldn't move."

Rainey laughed. "I guess Danny and I should eat before we go home then. You two probably won't be hungry for a bit."

Katie's voice brightened, when she asked, "Are you on your way now?"

"Not quite yet. Danny and I are going to check a few details in Chance's story, and then we'll be home."

Katie said, "We are leaving the restaurant now and should be home in about an hour. I have to take Ann home first. You're going to love the tiny houses. They made the safety changes you asked for. I can't wait for you to see them."

"How's the weather where you are?" Rainey asked, watching lightning flashes in the clouds near Durham.

"It looks nasty," Katie said. "We're in Chapel Hill. The wind has really picked up. We might be a little later getting home. I don't want to run into hail with the van. Ann said we can wait it out in one of the construction garages till it passes."

"Okay, honey," Rainey said. "I'll see you soon. Be careful."

"Are we still in mortal danger," Katie asked half kidding, but not really. It was another coping mechanism Katie used which required her to be flippant in times of stress.

"Just be aware that someone has made a threat. I'll fill you in when I see you."

"All right, then. We are in a watch, not a warning, conditions are favorable, be on the lookout. You be careful. I love you. See you soon. Oh, Cathleen says to tell Danny hello."

"He can hear you," Rainey said.

Cathleen's voice filled the car. "Hey, Danny. I tried Carolina barbecue, and I want a tiny house."

"We just bought a huge house," Danny said.

Cathleen came back with, "I've changed my mind and want to live in a tiny house in Rai-y an- Ka-ie's ba-yar-..."

Rainey saw the sky light up in the distance as the call dropped out.

An automated female voice purred, "Call ended."

"Remember, after Katrina when they voted down a bill requiring cell towers to have at least eight hours of battery power," Rainey said. "That is why when there is a power outage the strength of signal goes way down. The newer towers put in after 2007 usually have battery power, but the older network still hasn't been updated."

Rainey glanced over at Danny. He was staring at her, mouth opened a bit, an expression of wonder on his brow.

"What?" she asked.

"An unknowing person would guess that you simply have too much time to surf the Internet and read random shit. But I bet you have a legit reason for knowing that."

"As a matter of fact, I do. I had a case where the suspect's cell phone said he was not at the crime scene when a witness saw a man throw a woman from a third story balcony. A storm knocked out power and cell service to his carrier in the area of the crime scene. It turned out to be a stroke of luck on his part that he received a call while committing the crime. Phone records placed his phone nearer to the next cell tower, which happened to cover the apartment he rented for his mistress. He was just that lucky."

"So, how did you prove he did it?"

Rainey chuckled. "I didn't. His mistress gave him up and testified that he couldn't believe the power outage was giving him an alibi and how it had cost him nothing to get away with killing 'that bitch.' The mistress cost more, and he didn't pay up."

Danny sighed. "Alas, we don't have a mistress to give up Chance."

"But we do have The Inquisitive Mistress, Vanessa Wilhelm. Pull up what Brooks sent on her. I just scanned all that stuff. Did you see those blog entries Brooks highlighted? The Mistress interviewed a lot of Hale Trucking employees."

Danny busily opened and closed windows on the computer, zeroing in on pertinent info.

"I see that she said retired Special Agent Rainey Bell refused an interview."

"I don't remember the request. Ernie could have played gatekeeper on that one. She knows I don't discuss cases I worked while at the Bureau with anyone outside the FBI."

Rainey gripped the wheel a little tighter and focused on the road as the wind buffeted the car, rocking the laptop in its holder. They caught up with the rain on the backside of the storm. Rainey turned on the windshield wipers.

Danny braced the laptop with his hand so he could continue to read.

"Wilhelm also spoke with Eugene H. Berry, son of Jean Berry. Eugene said his mother could not be interviewed because of dementia. Yet, Wilhelm notes Jean Berry is still signing checks, which she discovered by chatting up a teller down at the bank. The teller said Ms. Berry still came to the bank herself on rare occasions, but he assured Vanessa, Jean Berry does not have dementia. She's sharp and no one to be trifled with."

Rainey slowed the car more as the rain fell harder. Her thought processes decelerated with it. Taking the cue from her body, Rainey took a deep breath and released it with the anxiousness that felt as though it was freezing her brain.

Danny commented, "Wow, that was a hell of a stress release. You good now."

"Yes. I got it in my head that we had to see this woman. I think I just asked myself why."

Danny didn't want to talk about her processes, which Rainey adored about him. He answered her question. "Okay, we know the IP address is tied to an account paid for by Jean Berry at her residence on Station Road. Chance could still have set this up. Hijack the Wi-Fi from outside and send whatever from whomever and it will look like it originated here. Brooks said the tablet identification data traces back to Vanessa Wilhelm. Vanessa's family said the one she carried for interviews is missing."

Rainey listened to yet another circumstantial evidence-laden saga in the Chance Hale tale.

"They are the only people left," Rainey said. "Jean and Eugene are it. Everyone else is dead except Robby."

She exchanged a quick look with Danny.

"We need to know for sure Robby is out of circulation," Danny said and began typing into the laptop immediately. "Brooks can nail that down for us." He hit the enter key with some flourish, saying, "Okay, what next?"

"We have twenty minutes to come up with a reason that Jean Berry or her son, Eugene, could be the masterminds of a serial murder run two decades long, able to stop at will and pick up again if the need arises. What kind of crimes are these? What's the payoff for the killer?"

Danny added his own questions, "What do the victims have in common? What nerve did Vanessa Wilhelm hit, or rather who did she unnerve?"

Rainey gave consideration to a theory she had never given much credence. "Could this person have hidden in the edges of Chance Hale's life? Is this someone that was never on anyone's radar, not even Chance's, whom I have assumed knows more than he's saying." Rainey popped the steering wheel with the heel of her hand for emphasis, saying, "Or is he the calculating killer I've always thought he was? If he is, he has a partner. That partner is the person I want to talk to."

The incoming caller alert sounded. "You have an incoming call from Brooks."

Rainey pushed the button on the steering wheel, answering the call, "Our Ms. Brooks, tell me crime solving clues so we can wrap this day up and go watch young men fly through the air, dropping threes like rain."

"I am recording every moment. Don't tell me any scores," Brooks said. She and Rainey shared a love of tournament time.

Danny asked, "Do you have the email I just sent?"

Rainey could hear Brooks' fingernails clicking against her keyboard as she answered the questions posed to her, "I do have that email and was way ahead of you on that one. It occurred to me that elimination of family members and employees as suspects was our challenge here."

"You are Magic Melatiah after all," Rainey remarked.

Brooks chuckled. "No magic at all. These people are just like any other criminal; they want something somebody else has, and they take it. It's like Hannibal Lector said—people covet."

Danny teased, "Oh no, you're not quoting Hannibal, are you?"

"Tell me he's wrong," Brooks countered. "It doesn't matter what excuse or reason these serial killers give you for their crimes, it all boils down to they took because they wanted a thing someone else had, be it money or self-worth. That's coveting."

Rainey steered the car around a significant ponding of rainwater on the highway, while she said to Danny, "She has a point."

The horizon lit up the eerie green hue that signifies a transformer struck by lightning in the distance. The rumble of thunder filled the car.

Rainey warned, "We're driving into a severe storm so the call could drop. Tell us the important stuff first."

Brooks began the information dump. "First, Robby Hughes is in a long-term care facility. He can walk and talk, but he has a way to go and may never fully recover. His guardian is Jean Berry."

A great BOOM interrupted Brooks, as lightning made contact with the earth somewhere nearby.

"Good Lord, is all hell breaking loose down there?"

Danny spoke over the noise, "Rainey insists we drive into a severe thunderstorm, so that's what we're doing."

Rain began to roar against the roof of the car in rhythmic sheets. Thunder clapped directly after the lightning flashes, now coming with more frequency. They caught the main storm at Durham, ten minutes from Jean Berry's house on a clear day, but not today. Traffic snarled to a near stall.

Danny spoke to Brooks again, "Keep talking. That way I can't concentrate on the fact we're surrounded by so much electricity the hair is standing on my arms."

Rainey focused on the worsening road conditions and the five lanes of shiny red brake lights in front of her. Danny turned up the volume on the call and made notes.

Brooks continued, "All right, then. Now, follow me, children. When Joshua Hale blew up in North Dakota, Obadiah H. Hale already acted as Chance Hale's legal guardian. Less than a year later, after Obadiah's death, the court named Jean B. Berry his guardian. She was also the executor of Obadiah Hale's estate. Robert A. Hughes took over Hale Trucking management on paper, but Jean, a twenty percent stockholder, ran the business. Through the years, both Chance and Robby borrowed money from Jean, using their shares in Hale Trucking as collateral. When they couldn't pay back the loans, Jean claimed their shares until she eventually owned eighty-five percent of old Obadiah's empire. She even foreclosed on Robby's home there on the property. Her son owns the remaining fifteen percent. Robby and Chance have nothing left."

"Smart business woman or shark, none of that is illegal," Danny said. "What happened to Hale Trucking? It's no longer in business, right?"

"There was a sell-off of most of the equipment and vehicles in January of 2010. The land, houses, and buildings remain under Jean Berry's ownership through her company Löwenherz Industries, LLC. That corporation has spawned multiple businesses, all of which pay lease fees back to the mother company for operating space. Several of these firms made substantial purchases from the Hale Trucking sale at hugely discounted prices. Significant losses over here are covered by gains over there. This woman knows tax law and how to get around it."

Danny asked, "Can you tell if Jean Berry is still actively running her businesses?"

"Her signature is on a recent application to the Orange County zoning board to allow rental of parking spots for tiny houses on her property. She appeared in person, with a valid ID."

Rainey commented, "College kids are begging for places to park tiny houses. That's a hot income producer right now. Jean doesn't sound like a woman suffering from dementia."

"Why would Gee lie to Vanessa about his mother's health? It would be so easy to check," Danny said.

"Speaking of Gee," Brooks said, "Eugene H. Berry is absolutely squeaky clean. His credit is great, he pays his bills on time, and he's never had a speeding ticket. On paper, he is paid by Löwenherz Industries, but I can't tell you what Eugene does for a living. He pays his taxes and donates money to animal welfare causes. Something is definitely wrong with this guy. No one is that good. I could dig up dirt on the Pope but not this guy."

Rainey changed lanes and exited onto US 70 toward Eno. She pointed out the window to the north and said, "The Tammy Gaskill assault took place just north of here in the park. Fews Ford is an easy walking distance for OB Hale's boys, less than three miles."

"Speaking of the Gaskill case," Brooks said, "I found her in Richmond if you want to talk to her."

Danny added a piece of information. "Sheila said Ms. Gaskill was unwilling to help in the investigation."

Rainey was undeterred. "If we get the DNA match, even if the statute of limitations has passed, North Carolina courts have applied the discovery rule in some sexual abuse cases involving minors. Tammy Gaskill was barely fourteen-years-old at the time of her assault."

Brooks interjected, "You would force her to participate, even if she didn't want to? That's a second rape right there."

Rainey defended her statement. "No, of course not. What I'm saying is Ms. Gaskill may finally have the DNA evidence to back up her story, and if that changes her mind about prosecuting the offender, then great. If it allows her to put away any doubts she may have about what actually happened to her, that's much better."

The tink-tink-tink of hail pellets hitting the car commenced right as Rainey turned onto University Station Road. The tops of the trees whipped around, tossing leaves and small branches into the wind. Shredded by hail and knotted together by violent gusts, various types of greenery fell in wet clumps on the Charger's windshield. A heavy deluge added another degree of difficulty to clearly seeing the road. Rainey slowed the car to a crawl. They were inside the squall line.

"Damn, did the bottom drop out?" Brooks called over the howl of wind driving rain and hail into the exterior of the car.

The sun had yet another hour before its setting, but darkness fell all around them, while a staccato strobe of lightning danced across the sky. The ground under the car rumbled long after the flash and crash of the strike.

Much like when her dad would say, "Turn the radio down. I can't see for hearin' too much," Rainey dismissed Brooks.

"Hey, I'll call you back," she yelled over the deafening rumble.

Before she could disconnect, Rainey heard the automated voice say, "Call ended."

"Hey, unplug my laptop from the car," she said, peering through the windshield in hopes of catching a glimpse of the centerline.

"I thought you said we were safe in the car," Danny complained while pulling the charger cord out of the laptop.

"We are," Rainey explained, "but it can fry electronics if we get a direct hit."

Lightning streaked in front of the car and slammed into a tall pine tree next to the road. The top of the tree exploded, sending sparks flying. The sound of the atmosphere ripping joined the exploding pine to rattle the car and its occupants.

"Shit!" The expletive left both Danny and Rainey at the same time.

"If I could find somewhere to pull off the road, I would, but I can't see the shoulder."

"Next time, we listen to the weather report and heed the warnings," Danny retorted.

Rainey could see the tree line open up ahead.

"There's the overpass just ahead. I can pull off and let this clear. I don't want to go over I-85 with winds this high."

"I appreciate your showing a bit of caution, now that we're in the middle of the damn storm," Danny said.

Rainey took advantage of a flash of lightning to locate the wide paved shoulder before the overpass. As she pulled the car to a stop, she turned to Danny.

"I am sorry. I forgot storms made you nervous."

"You did not forget," Danny said.

"Well, since I've had to convince three children the world is not coming to an end when it storms, I had forgotten a grown man might have a panic attack," Rainey said, trying not to laugh.

The wind rocked the car, lightning tore through the air overhead, hail just a little shy of the size of golf balls slammed into the hood. Rainey saw Danny flinch as an especially large clump of ice smashed into the windshield.

She reassured him, "It's ballistic glass. Ice won't break it."

Danny eyed her with mock scorn. "I don't give you shit about your issues."

"What issues?" Rainey asked.

"How about when you hear someone throw up? Ble-eck," Danny made exaggerated puking sounds.

The sky lit for several seconds, a sustained lightning strike turned the dark into day. Across the bridge overpass, a giant billboard caught Rainey's attention.

"Did you see that?" she asked.

"See what?"

Rainey pointed at the billboard. "Watch over there. Wait for the lightning."

The lightning came quickly, held fast, and allowed a full perusal of the sign.

Rainey threw the car into gear and stomped on the gas. Hail exploded against the windshield as the Charger crossed the overpass. Rainey did not care about a gust of wind sweeping them off the bridge anymore.

As they passed the billboard, Rainey mumbled under her breath, "Son of a bitch."

Danny read the sign aloud, "Tiny Hart Living – We put a lot of heart in our tiny homes. Take Next Right."

17

At the end of a spacious parking lot, lightning flashes revealed two enormous steel garages standing like guardians to the forest behind them.

"What do you want to do?" Rainey asked.

She had stopped the Charger a few feet into the parking lot, under the shadow of a clump of trees. Danny peered through the rain at the buildings. The hail core had moved through, leaving broken limbs and power outages in its wake.

"Well, they know we're coming. I'm pretty sure of that," Danny said.

"Who is they?" Rainey asked. "Is it Hart and his wife, Ann Burke? Is it Jean and Eugene Berry? Is it all of them. I've seen Jean Berry, albeit nearly twenty years ago, and all I can tell you is she was a redhead and looked like a young Lucille Ball. I didn't get a great look at Ann behind the scarf and those huge sunglasses, but she is a brunette."

"So was Lucy's and dye is cheap," Danny said.

"Good point," Rainey said, "but still, that would take brass balls to come face to face with me. Besides, Jean would be in her sixties now. "

"How old do you think Ann is?"

Rainey shook her head. "I have no idea. You saw her, what do you think?"

Danny shrugged and asked another question. "How did Katie find this company to build the tiny houses?"

"Ann came to the shelter. She said she thought it would be a good idea to construct tiny houses for women in need and they were willing to do a build-one-get-one-free deal with no design strings attached."

"Sounds innocent enough," Danny commented.

"Or too much of a coincidence that they do business on former Hale property," Rainey countered.

Danny tried logic. "It would be a good way for a business like this to get free publicity and a tax write off."

"Not buying it," Rainey said, resolutely.

"But you didn't check them out?"

"Katie complained that I never trust her to be smart enough to avoid trouble. So I stayed completely out of this project except for exchanging a few emails and design ideas."

"You're never going to listen to her again, are you?"

Rainey stared ahead at the garages, one of which likely held her kidnapped wife.

She answered Danny with one word, "Nope."

"And you never met Hart?"

"No, again. I have no idea who Hartwell Burke is."

Danny picked up the notepad he had thrown on the dash. "Wait a minute. That name, I know that name."

From inside his chest pocket, he pulled a small flashlight that Rainey would have bet a million dollars was there. Danny was a creature of habit. He flipped through the pages of his notes.

"Here it is," he said, pointing at the page. "Obadiah Hartwell Hale. I knew I'd seen that name before."

"Eugene H. Hale. What do you bet his middle name is Hartwell?"

"I think we have a winner," Danny said and threw the notepad back on the dashboard.

"We should call for back-up, don't you think?"

Danny held up his phone. "I tried. Try yours."

Rainey hit the call button on her steering wheel. "Call Katie."

"No signal detected," came the automated reply.

"This isn't a cell tower down. The power is out, judging by the street lights," Rainey said, "but we're still close enough to plenty of working ones to have a few bars. I think the signal is jammed. Hang on."

Rainey dug into the center console and came out with a black plastic square shaped device, resembling a digital timer.

"It's a cell phone jammer detector. It was a gag gift from Molly because she says I'm paranoid."

Rainey pressed the "On" button. A red indicator light began to flash on the unit, and the digital display read, "Detected."

130

"I'll be damned. It works," Rainey said. A wave of dread crashed into her chest. "Well, now. That has all kinds of implications, doesn't it?"

Danny removed his weapon from its holster, checked the magazine, and then racked a round into the chamber. He asked, "Do we leave and get a signal or stay and walk into what is most assuredly a well thought out plan to get rid of the four of us?"

"Send Brooks an email. It's worth a shot. The Hotspot might connect to a random frequency the jammer isn't covering. It'll keep trying to connect as long as there is email in the outbox."

Rainey hit the switch that kept her interior light from coming on. With her headlights on the bright setting, she created the equivalent of a flashlight's blinding disorientation. It would be difficult for someone in the garages to discern who she was or what she was doing. After activating the latch release for the trunk, she opened the driver's side door and slid out into the slowing rain, calling over to Danny as she went, "When you're done, meet me at the back of the car."

Rainey took off the long duster and put on the windbreaker she kept in the car with the words "Bail Agent" in large yellow letters on the back. If cops were coming, she wanted to make damn sure they could identify the good guys. She grabbed a Bell's Bail and Investigations hat and slid it over her wet curls, giving some relief from the rain.

After opening the gun safe welded into the trunk floor, Rainey grabbed several magazines for the Glock she had tucked back in her holster after leaving the prison. She took out the shotgun she kept stored in the safe and opened a box of shells. After making sure the shotgun was fully loaded with one in the chamber, she filled her windbreaker pockets with the remaining shells. Danny slinked around to the back of the car.

Rainey asked, "If you need more magazines for your Glock, there are two more in there."

"Are we just going in there guns blazing? We don't know that Katie and Cathleen are in there. They could be on the way home by now. We don't know if these people are guilty of anything other than sending a picture of you and your family to an inmate in a threatening email."

Rainey tilted her head and gave Danny her very best, "Are you serious?" expression.

"Yeah, okay," Danny said, "but the smart move here is to go get help. We don't know which garage to breach, do we?"

Rainey looked over the raised trunk lid to the garages one hundred yards away. A drop of icy rainwater trickled under her collar and down her spine. As if answering Danny's question, the entry door of the garage on the left opened slowly, revealing nothing but darkness inside.

Danny saw it too. He said, "I'll be damned."

"There's your sign, Agent McNally," Rainey said, handing him the old FBI baseball cap she kept in the trunk. "Here, so when the cops come, they won't shoot you."

"How will they know to come? We're gambling on that email going through."

"You go then," Rainey said. "Leave me here and go get help."

"I'm not leaving you. I'm just trying to raise the odds for Katie and Cathleen." He put his hand on Rainey's shoulder. "If we don't succeed, no one knows where we are."

Rainey had an epiphany. She smiled at Danny and reached into the trunk, where she removed a wrapped present and proceeded to open it like a child at Christmas. Once opened, she held up a handheld device, colored bright tennis ball yellow.

"Do you know what this is?"

Danny shook his head.

"This was to be Katie's next gift when I screwed up. By the way, you should stock those. Marriage tip."

"What is it?"

"This my friend," Rainey said as she pulled out the small antenna on the device, "this is a waterproof personal locator beacon that will set rescue in motion to this location in about five minutes from when I push this button. After that, we're about ten minutes outside Hillsborough. If everything goes as advertised, we should have help in fifteen minutes."

"Push the fucking button, Rainey."

Rainey grinned. "I put batteries in it already. Good thing I believe in being prepared. That's not paranoia, by the way."

"Jesus, you're killing me. Push the damn button," Danny said.

Rainey pushed the button and put the device on the pavement behind them. "This will bring them close enough."

Danny wiped the rain from the bill of his cap. "By the way, I might have had bad luck with women, but even I know that is a shitty gift. I don't think I'll be taking marriage tips from you."

Rainey said, "She'll love it if it saves her ass," and meant it, while she slid her ballistic vest over the windbreaker. "I'm sorry, I don't have two vests back here, but you'll be inside the car. It's a giant bulletproof vest. Just stay in it."

Rainey closed the gun safe and made sure it was locked. She grabbed a flashlight out of the trunk and checked to see that it worked.

Danny adjusted the hat to fit his head and then stuffed the two magazines in his jacket pockets, rechecked his weapon, and asked, "If I'm in the car, where will you be?"

Rainey smiled, "Combat tactics, Agent McNally. Since I don't have any flash/bang grenades to cover my entry, you are going to be my noisy distraction."

#

Rainey slipped into the shadows of the surrounding forest and made her way southward around the parking lot.

"Why don't I go look in the window?" Danny had asked.

"Because my vest will not fit you," Rainey argued.

She crept toward the garage, setting her sights on the windows lining the south side of the building. The sun had now slipped below the horizon. The trailing wispy gray clouds they left in Butner arrived. The worst of the storm had passed. It wasn't completely dark, but it was still hard to see. Thunder rolled overhead, but the lightning merely flickered in the sky. Rainey couldn't use the flashlight for fear of giving away her position. She moved as quickly as she could without slipping on the patches of accumulated hail and dead falls littering the forest floor.

Rainey advanced like her father had taught her. A few deliberate, slow steps and then listen, a few more steps, listen. She kept her eyes on the building, watching for movement. Danny inched the car closer to the garage, cautiously, trying to draw attention away from Rainey. She stayed out of the glow of the headlights, moving parallel to the structure until she felt she could cross to one of the windows safely.

"Okay, Rainey," she said to herself, "go get your girl."

Hoping she wouldn't be shot the moment she exposed herself, Rainey darted from the cover of the trees to squat under the closest window to the door. Danny dimmed the lights on the car, a prearranged signal to let her know he saw her make the move. He then began to drive in a wide sweeping circle in front of the garage, in an attempt to keep the person in the garage focused on the car.

When the headlights moved from the garage, Rainey took the chance to peek in through the window. The plan was for Rainey to make sure that Cathleen and Katie were not positioned behind the garage door. The plan went awry when Rainey bobbed up and down one too many times, trying to get a good look inside the garage. On the third look-see, Rainey met the face of a man staring back at her.

She had not seen anyone in the garage, but then only a battery operated emergency exit sign shed any light on the dark interior. At the moment she met the face in the window, Danny completed the wide circle and again aimed the car at the big roll-up bay door. The beam of one of the headlights shined into the garage where the smaller door stood open. It bathed the man on the other side of the window in harsh white light. He ducked out of sight just as Rainey leveled the shotgun at his face. She didn't see much of him, but she saw the red hair and beard.

"Eugene."

Rainey sprinted toward the open door. Danny, seeing this, jammed on the accelerator. The Charger's rear wheels squealed and smoked as rubber caught the pavement and shot the car forward. Rainey's car could go from zero to sixty miles per hour in less than five seconds. It only took three seconds for it to crash through the roll-up door and into the garage. The door folded over the car forming a Charger taco. Danny didn't let off the gas until he had sideswiped the tiny house parked a few feet inside the doorway and rammed a weighty standing toolbox straight ahead. The crushed door reflected the car's headlights in dust-filled beams of light shooting in multiple directions, which offered little help with the darkness of the huge garage.

Rainey entered a second behind the car, bolting through the door with the shotgun raised, prepared to take out any threat. She cleared the corner behind her and kept her back to it, as she scanned the inky blackness beyond the scene of the crash.

She did not see the man but yelled into the shadowy abyss where she sensed more than saw movement, "Get on the ground. Get on the ground. Let me see your hands."

The response, a muzzle flash, came instantly. Rainey crouched and returned one round with the shotgun before she rolled behind the Charger. The brake lights lit her up like a Christmas tree. Danny attempted to get out of the car, his efforts blocked by part of the garage door.

Rainey yelled to him, "Danny, turn the car off. Take your foot off the brake."

The car went silent. The brake lights blinked off. Now the glare of the headlamps prevented seeing beyond the car.

"Headlights. Kill the headlights."

She heard Danny yell, "Where's the switch?"

BANG! PING! Another bullet whizzed by Rainey, hitting the mangled steel above her head.

"Left of the steering wheel, on the bottom edge of the console. Spin the dial until the lights go out."

Mercifully, the lights went out after a few seconds. The cavernous space glowed red near the front exit. Rainey peeked toward the back of the garage. She could see another glowing exit sign casting a red hue over the rear door. BANG! PING! This time the sound was closer. Rainey dropped to her stomach and peered under the car. The crushed roll-up door blocked her view. She placed the shotgun on the floor and pulled the Glock from its holster.

She could feel the Charger moving as Danny climbed around inside, trying to find a way out. Rainey slid over to the passenger side of the car, where it rested against the tiny house. She thought she heard someone inside the house, but the sound of footsteps running toward the back of the garage needed her immediate attention.

In an instant, Rainey was on her feet. When the silhouette of a man appeared in the red glow of the exit light, she fired two shots.

BAM! BAM!

The first shot broke a pane of glass out of the window in the door. The second shot hit the man in the shoulder. He stumbled forward and pushed through the exit so hard the door rebounded and slammed shut.

Rainey heard Danny finally roll out of the driver's side passenger door.

She called out to him, "Shooter exited the rear of the building."

Danny slid around to the back of the car and kneeled down beside Rainey. "Do you think he was alone?" he asked.

Rainey didn't answer. She was distracted by sounds coming from inside the tiny house.

She raised a fist in the air, silently telling Danny to stop talking and stay still.

A muffled voice broke the silence, calling out, "Rainey!"

"That's Katie. She's in the tiny house," Rainey whispered. "Watch my back."

Danny stood up into a shooting crouch, eyes focused on the back of the garage. Rainey stepped over the tongue of the trailer holding the tiny house. The doors to the utility storage locker built into the end of the structure stood open. She could see the water heater and propane tank inside. Something else caught her eye as the window above the storage locker filled with Katie and Cathleen's faces.

"Rainey, thank God," Katie shouted.

Rainey knew the plans for this house. She had reviewed them and suggested the window where Cathleen and Katie were as an egress point, meaning it could be opened and used as an emergency exit if needed. Rainey thought this qualified as an emergency.

"Open the window," Rainey said.

Cathleen responded with an adamant, "We can't."

Thinking the window was stuck, Rainey told the two women, "Stand back. I'll break it."

Both women inside the tiny house screamed, "No," simultaneously.

"Why not?" Rainey asked, confused by their insistence.

With remarkable calmness, considering what she had to say, Cathleen explained, "There is a bomb hooked to the propane tank. The guy said he added C-4 to make sure there wouldn't be anything left of us to find."

Rainey took a step back and refocused on the utility locker, realizing the thing that caught her attention was a digital read out on an improvised explosive device. It was blinking one word over and over, "Armed."

"Holy shit," escaped her lips before she could catch it.

She looked back up at Cathleen and Katie and forced a smile.

"Let's just get you out of there and let the bomb squad deal with this."

Cathleen shook her head. "It's tied into the security system. Any attempt to open a door or window will trigger the device." She sighed, and then added, "Unfortunately, as he explained, it also has a timer that would go off if the device isn't activated or reset in the next," she paused to think before finishing, "I believe we have about ten minutes left, fifteen tops."

Danny appeared at Rainey's side.

He said, "With all the noise you guys are making, if there was anybody else in here, they know where to shoot." He looked up at Cathleen and Katie. "Hi, honey. Do you want to rethink hanging out with these two," he joked.

Nobody laughed. Rainey pointed at the IED.

"We've got a big problem."

"Oh, shit," breathed from Danny's lips.

Cathleen began speaking, "I need one of you to take a picture with your cell phone and show it to me."

Rainey guessed her surprise read in her expression, because Cathleen responded, "Captain Augustine, 303rd Explosives Ordinance Disposal Battalion, Schofield Barracks, Hawaii."

Katie nodded. This was not new information for her. Evidently, the two women had discussed this aspect of Cathleen's background. It was news to Rainey but welcomed.

"I told you she is not without skills," Danny said, already holding his phone out to take images of the device. "I'll take a few from different angles."

He leaned in for the pictures. Rainey peeked around the side of the tiny house and watched the rest of the garage, as the strobe from the camera briefly illuminated the space. Katie's van was parked in the next bay. Rainey noticed the loft upstairs and wondered if that trunk of porn magazines was still there, or worse, another killer. The rear exit door swung back and forth in the draft created by the sizeable hole in the front of the garage. Thinking it has slammed shut before, it drew her attention.

"Stay behind the house," she told Danny. Then she asked Katie through the glass, "Where is Ann?"

"She let us into the garage out of the hail and said she needed to go check on her cat. She never came back. Hart came in and, well, the rest is self-explanatory."

"So Hart Burke did this," Rainey said, looking for verification.

"Yes," Katie answered, "but I don't understand it. He was always so sweet."

Cathleen asked for attention after reviewing the photos in Danny's phone, which he held up to the window for her.

"Okay, Hart had a phone in his hand and said all he had to do was dial a number and boom."

"That wouldn't work," Rainey said. "There is a cell phone jammer turned on somewhere on this property."

Cathleen's expression read incredulous, as if she were about to explain something basic to a recruit, when she said, "Rainey, if it can be turned on, it can be turned off. Go find him."

Katie pushed her face as close to the glass as she could. Rainey jumped on the trailer tongue and mirrored Katie, so close to the glass it began to fog.

Katie said, "Honey, we can't both be in this garage."

Rainey stared into Katie's blue eyes and asked, "Cathleen, what if we take the siding off or cut a hole in the bottom."

Katie pressed her hand to the windowpane. "Rainey, he thought of all those things. You thought of all those things. There are sensors in the walls, floor, and ceiling. The floor is made with a Kevlar lining. The walls have bullet resistant drywall. It's a tiny tank, we're locked inside, and you can't be here. You have to go. Our kids can't lose us both."

Cathleen had always reflected quiet calm. She laughed easily and went with the flow of things, but not today.

"Screw that," she said. "I'm not dying in a tiny house. You," she pointed at Rainey, "go find that asshole and take his phone. You," she pointed at Danny, "you're going to need tools. Find pliers, wire cutters, and grab all the little screwdrivers you can find. A sharp knife would help."

Rainey still standing on the tongue of the trailer looked down at Danny. "If you can get to the keys, everything you need is in my trunk."

"Go find him, Rainey. You're our safety net."

Rainey turned back to Katie. "I'll be back to get you. I love you."

"I love you, too. Be safe Rainey Blue Bell."

"Always."

18

The Grotto

"Remember Rainey, a wounded man will run until he can't, and then he will lie down to die or coil up and prepare to fight to the death. The problem is both of those things look a lot alike right up until they don't. A nearly dead man can still kill you."

Billy Bell's warning sounded in Rainey's head, as her flashlight beam landed on drops of blood on the foliage leading into the forest behind the garage. She crouched in the undergrowth at the base of a large Tulip tree, with her flashlight low to the ground and the beam pointed straight down in front of her. The man she shot had stopped to lean against this tree. Trickled trails of softly falling raindrops ran through his bloody handprint, staining the gray tree bark red.

In front of her, three worn paths diverged from the back of the garage. These trails had been in use for many years. Rainey reflected on Danny's description of the satellite images of the property. Jean Berry's home lay to the north on a gravel path beyond the end of Station Road. The footpath leading in that direction had been used daily. The house on the south side of the property had once belonged to Robby Hughes. The path leading toward it was less trafficked with new growth extending into the trail. The third track had seen extensive use and bore the traces of a hand-truck or wheelbarrow. This was a supply line and led toward the westerly edge of the property and the grotto.

Rainey turned off the flashlight. She took a deep breath in through her nose and let it out slowly her mouth. She did this several times until she felt the adrenaline rush recede enough that her heartbeat no longer filled her ears. Now, she could hear the forest around her. Rain dropped through the trees, from leaf to leaf. The tops of the tall pines creaked in the trailing breeze of the storm. Freshly sheared vegetation scattered across the forest floor demonstrated hail's destructive power.

Rainey was running out of time. She had to get moving, but which way? The woods were not quiet, especially after a violent spring storm. Once the all clear sounded from the first brave souls, the rest of the insects and frogs found their full-throated evening voices, seeking hookups and reunions as life continued on. Nature's song reverberated under the thick tree canopy of new seasonal growth. Even so, the snap of a twig underfoot stuck out as unnatural. He was there, moving away from her, headed west toward the grotto.

#

Rainey and Katie took the kids to the North Carolina Zoo last summer. Timothy's love of animals extended to the wilds of Africa. The lion enclosure brought on an excited discussion with a zookeeper who had the patience to answer a million questions from three excited four-year-olds.

Inside the sunny, open-air exhibit, a lioness sunbathed on a rock outcropping with her cubs. A huge male with a long flowing mane lounged in the grass not far away. Rainey remembered looking at the paw of the big guy and understanding exactly why he was called the King of the Jungle. One of the facts the zookeeper shared with the kids stood out in Rainey's mind at the moment. The keeper said an average adult male lion would weigh four hundred and twenty pounds. An average female was much smaller at two hundred and eighty pounds.

After hearing a lion roar in close proximity to her location in a dark, thick, and unfamiliar forest, Rainey whispered under her breath, "I hope that's a female. More importantly, I hope that is a female that cannot get to me."

She could hear her little naturalist Timothy comment in her head, "But Nee Nee, the lioness is the main hunter."

"Thanks, for the info bud," her inner voice answered back.

Not recognizing the guttural grunting sound at first, Rainey's brain said, "HIDE," which she did. A distinctive roar followed the series of grunts. Rainey identified the sound about the time she landed in the wet leaves behind a stack of fallen logs. Timothy's animal obsession had extended into his fifth year. A CD of the "Sounds of Africa" and its accompanying book ranked as two of his prized possessions, right up there with Carl, the dog. Rainey was familiar with the communication methods of elephants, gorillas, chimpanzees, water buffalo, baboons, wildebeests, and more, but the one she would recognize above all others was Timothy's favorite—the call of Africa, the roar of a lion.

At the first grunt, she had ducked behind the stack of dead falls outside the ten-foot chain-link fence she nearly plowed into. It was covered with vines so dense she couldn't see through to what the fence was guarding.

"Raawwwrrr," echoed from behind the fence.

A man's voice demanded, "Hey, hey. Get back there."

The voice lacked command tenor. It was more a suggestion than an order. Rainey was not the only animal who sensed the speaker's weakness.

"Raawwrr," came the answer.

Next were the sounds of whining hinges and the groaning of a heavy metal door grinding shut with a reverberating thunk. These were audible reminders to any creature that had ever heard them, including man, that freedom was not theirs to have. As uncomfortable as the sound made the animal, it alarmed Rainey quite a bit.

"Let's hope that was the lion being shut in and not let out," she whispered.

Talking to herself helped keep the anxiety of thinking about being attacked by a lion at bay. But talking, even whispering, was ill advised with a predator nearby. It was best to keep her thoughts audibly unexpressed.

"Well, that explains the bite marks on the skulls. Let's not add your own to the collection," she thought while studying her surroundings.

She was at a corner in the fencing. As she peeked around the stack of logs, Rainey could see a gate on the fence. A gate, which a quick check with her flashlight proved, left open with a bloody palm print visible on the vertical bracing.

"Okay, now that's a clue."

The growling and roaring had stopped. No more doors creaked or groaned. The dripping of rain and nature's chorus resumed its audible dominance. Knowing she had no choice but to follow, Rainey stood and approached the gate. The voice she had heard, and the lion roars seemed to come from deep inside a cavernous space, giving her the confidence that there was some distance and possibly a structure between the entrance and the source. She slid through the opening without touching it, avoiding any creaking warnings to the occupants inside.

A dim amber light shone through a small, square doorway at the back of the grotto. Too short for a human to walk through without stooping low to the ground, the opening provided enough ambient light for Rainey to see shadows and thankfully the steep drop off below the observation platform where she stood. The entire structure was made of stone or had been created to look that way. A massive back wall stood about thirty feet away. It and the sides attached to it were about eight feet taller than the front wall that formed the concrete deck for peering down at the animal on the floor of the enclosure, about eighteen feet below.

"This does not look like the exhibit we saw at the zoo."

The depth of the enclosure explained the muffled cavernous quality of the noises. It had come from an interior space, where the glow allowing Rainey to see originated. The opening permitted the animal inside to explore its stone prison under a limited view of the sky. There was no hope of ever scaling the steep walls, not by man or beast, not without a rope, which Rainey did not have.

Above the outside fencing, a labyrinth of steel piping created a dome of wire and vines. It resembled a giant birdcage plopped down over the grotto like a cloche over the main course. It reached at least twenty feet into the surrounding canopy of old growth forest. Rain dripped through the wire mesh. Sunlight could filter in, but whatever lived beneath the tangle of vines and steel had not seen the wide-open sky for many years.

"This is looking very Jurassic Parky."

Before leaving the garage, Rainey had crawled through her car to reach the console, where she retrieved the cell signal jammer detector. She pulled it out now, verifying the jammer was still activated.

"I hope you have my girl out of that garage by now, McNally," she whispered under her breath while shoving the device back into her pocket. "I'm going to kiss your future wife if she disables that bomb."

She started looking for a way down to the level where Eugene/Hart had gone. Guessing the best place to start was down the fence line, Rainey felt for it in the shadows. Something or someone passed the little doorway below, temporarily blocking the light. It became creepy dark in that instant. Her brain remembered the drop-off, sending a wave of unsteadiness to remind her to watch her step. Gripping the fence to stave off a stumble, the chain-link let out a rusty groan under her weight.

Rainey froze against the fence and listened for a reaction. The sound of shuffling footsteps below told her it wasn't a lion on the loose down there. She remembered watching a nature show with Timothy, where, in a thick South African accent, the guide told his guests, "Don't worry so much at every twig snapping. It is the animal you do not hear that will get you. If the lion wants to eat you, he will make no sound until the second before you are about to be his meal."

A bi-pedal animal, a human, skidded lightly across the stone floor. That was no man. At least not one the size of the guy she put a bullet in. *"Childlike,"* her brain spit out to a woman who knew the sound of children skittering about.

"Think, Rainey," she said in a hushed breath.

Who had she not accounted for? Ann was Hart/Eugene's wife. Did she know who he really was? Rainey knew plenty of wives of serial

141

murderers that had no clue to whom they were married. She also knew plenty who played an active part in their husbands' crimes.

Whether it was Ann, Jean, or both in the bowels of the grotto, Rainey thought, *"If a bloody man didn't scare you out of there, you're either unable to leave or complicit."*

She inched along the fence until she came to a metal door, this one large enough for a person. It had to be the way in. The ticking of the clock in her head told her she had to go. Rainey pulled on the handle before the fear could stop her.

The creak was slight, explaining why she hadn't heard it earlier when Eugene went down these steps. She couldn't see the bottom of the stairs because they curved, but she knew he was down there. There was no doubt. Rainey could see bloody handprints smeared along one of the dimly lit walls of the stairway. There was also no doubt that her presence had been detected.

Eugene's weakening voice called out, "Naamah? What took you tho long?" His lisp evident on the "s," soft "c," "sh," and "z" sounds, which were replaced with "th," he explained his predicament, "I'm thot. I need help. I dropped the jammer remote thomewhere. I can't get to the unit to turn it off manually. I can't activate the IED. They're going to get away and call the polithe. We have to run."

The lisp confirmed his identity and that he was waiting for his mommy.

"How utterly predictable, Rainey thought, *"a serial killer with self-esteem and mother issues."*

Rainey focused on the part where he said he dropped the jammer remote and couldn't activate the IED. Maybe he lied about the necessity for a reset.

Eugene struggled to move around. That was the scene Rainey's brain imagined while listening to his strained grunts and heavy breathing, as he continued speaking.

"I rethet it when they pulled up. They have about thirty minuteth left on the timer. They'll ethcape if they haven't already. We need to get out of here. Help me get her ready."

"Raawrr. Hiss-ss."

His feet could be heard shuffling across the cement floor, as Eugene spoke to someone or something beyond Rainey's view.

"Back up. What'th wrong with you?"

Rainey was a bit more concerned about the lion than the man with the gun. On the bright side, she knew Jean wasn't down there with Eugene, and Cathleen had more time to disable the device than originally thought. It also meant Jean was mobile and mentally aware enough to know what a jammer was and to make it down the steep staircase. Jean was also conscious of the bomb. Apparently, her son anticipated his mother coming to help him.

Rainey didn't need ol' Jean sneaking in behind her. She pulled the door shut and looked for a latch, but found none.

"I suppose it wasn't built to keep people out," she thought.

Her next thought ran around in her brain screaming, *"Shit, shit, shit. I'm going to get locked in if I go down there."*

Rainey pushed the door open a few inches. It squeaked a bit, but not as much as before. Her worry over the noise was drowned out by her sudden appreciation for the crisp, fresh air being drawn in. The door was massive and made heavy steel. Feeling around in her pockets for a way to jam the door open, she found the shotgun shells she had stuffed there. She took two out and wedged them into the long hinge that ran the length of the door.

"Now the door can't close. One problem solved breeds another. I can't shut the door either, and I'm exposing my back to whoever pulls it open."

Rainey would have to deal with Jean if the time came, but at the moment the pressing issues were Eugene, the lion, and whoever else was down there. She pressed her back against the wall and began her descent into the unknown.

"Naamah?" Eugene called out again.

"Nope, not your mommy," Rainey said aloud.

Rainey crept down the steps, curving with the wall as she progressed, and trying to get an idea of where Eugene might be. The cavern's rounded edges and uneven surfaces caused the sound to bounce around the enclosure.

"I have a gun," Eugene said.

"I'm aware of that," Rainey answered. "I have one too, but then you know that as well."

"Where ith Naamah?"

"She's not here. I think that is the most pertinent information at the moment. Would you like to know more?"

Eugene didn't answer the question. Rainey stopped before she reached the bottom step. She could see part of the smooth cement floor. She knew he would take a shot at her the second she stepped into view. Even with the vest on, Rainey had no desire to take a bullet, much less have him get lucky and accidentally shoot her where she was not protected.

"Here's what I know, Eugene. I know that you are injured and need to go to the hospital. I know that only people with badges are going to get around me to get to you. FYI, they're on the way. Your little jammer thingy rotates through signals. My personal locator beacon will hit on a satellite while your jammer is off blocking cell signals from bomb detonators. I also know that the IED is being handled by a bomb technician, you don't have the jammer, and I have a lot more bullets than you do."

"It...only...taketh...one," came a strained, staccato reply.

Eugene was trying to move and in pain.

"Look, there is no way I'm dying down here with you this evening. It's just not going to happen. You guys are all alike, you know. You think I sit around thinking about you all the time, hunting you, just waiting for the opportunity to face you in some life or death struggle. That's not even remotely true. I'm a fucking analyst, for Christ's sake."

"You're an FBI profiler," Eugene said, acknowledging that he knew who waited in the shadows for him.

"I was an FBI behavioral analyst and not the TV kind. I sat behind a desk reviewing case files. I walked crime scenes after the violence was long over. I interviewed assholes like you after they were safely behind bars. I wasn't running around in a ballistics vest leading raids on the lairs of serial killers. I have had more near death experiences since I've been out of the Bureau than my entire fifteen years in it. I don't intend to die at the hands of one of you miscreants because you felt the need to draw attention to yourself for whatever bizarre reason. So bleed to death you murdering ass-hat. I don't care. I'll sit right here and wait before I step around this wall and let you take another shot at me. Better yet, I should just lock you down here, go back to the garage, and wait for the police."

"You think I killed thothe women, but I didn't."

"Great, another of Obadiah Hale's sons is a wrongfully accused innocent man."

"My father wath an evil man."

That declaration confirmed what Rainey suspected. This whole thing was a family affair—a very sick family lacking in genetic diversity. The cleft palate was a clue to consanguinity in the bloodline. The fact that he was wielding a gun, trying to set off a bomb, and possibly a serial killer fell right in with family norms.

"I agree with you, based on what Chance has told me, but he also spawned at least two serial killers. Joshua is dead. That leaves you, Robby, and Chance. My money is on you, right now."

"He didn't kill them," a female voice joined the conversation.

"GRrrrrrr." A low growl rumbled through the grotto.

"Sich beruhigen. Es ist alles in Ordnung." The female voice comforted the lion in what Rainey recognized as German. From her very shaky remembrance of university language classes and a couple of trips overseas, she was pretty sure the lion was told to calm itself. The female addition to the conversation gave Rainey pause, but the lion's contribution reminded her there was more than one predator around the corner.

"If he didn't kill anyone, then he should put down the weapon and let me help him," Rainey said.

"You can't run any farther, Eugene. There is no other way out of here except those stairs. Let her help you."

Eugene answered, "We're going to die anyway."

"No one needs to die. We can end all of this right now. Just put down the weapon and slide it on the floor toward me. I'm not here to kill people. Despite what people have said about me, I don't like doing that sort of thing, really."

"He isn't talking about you. It's Naamah. He only does what she says so he can keep me alive."

"*Keep me*," Rainey thought. Did the voice belong to a captive? It wasn't Ann. Not unless she was masking her raspy delivery. It wasn't Jean either, from what Rainey remembered of their brief interaction. One thing had been hard to miss there in the Border Patrol office. That accent was unmistakable. The speaker in the grotto had no telltale Piedmont non-rhotic accent, where the "r" was dropped at the end of words. This person said "farther" with a strong "r." Jean would have said, "fathuh" instead.

Rainey asked the female, "What is your name?"

"Eve."

There was no one named Eve in the catalogue of victims in the Hale cases. Then again, Rainey only knew of three victims who had survived an encounter with one or more of the Hale men, Emily Dawson, Tammy Lynn Gaskill, and Donna Travis.

"Don't talk to her," Eugene said. "Get back away from there. Do it, or Naamah will punith all of uth. Juth wait. Naamah ith coming."

"Eve, my name is Rainey Bell. No matter what he's threatened you with or has told you will happen if you escape, none of it is true. You have to trust me. I can get you out of here. Just come to me. The door is open. We can walk out of here together. I promise you, I will keep you safe."

Eve didn't answer.

Eugene's weak plea of, "Don't lithen," and his labored breathing, when he said, "Can't help uth now," indicated his condition worsened quickly.

"Listen to him, Eve. He's fading fast. He's not going to make it if he doesn't get help soon. I can get that for him, but you have to come with me."

Waiting for Eve's answer took only seconds, but in the silence of the moment, it felt as if everything slowed and the sounds amplified.

Rainwater dripped on cement somewhere. A big cat panted. A man groaned. Her own heart raced against the time that crept by until she heard Eve make a request.

"Open the door, Eugene. Let me out."

Eugene sobbed. His near whisper of, "I'm dyin', Eve," faded with the saying of her name.

"You have to help. Come quick. Let me out."

Eve began her desperate cries, punctuated with what sounded like the rattling of a jail cell door. Familiar with the noise and knowing it meant Eve was locked behind bars; Rainey took a step and then stopped.

"How do I know you aren't lying and he isn't sitting there ready to shoot me when I gullibly come around that corner?"

"Please, help us. She'll kill us all."

Rainey leaned hard against the wall and weighed her options. Katie would be really pissed if she were killed for being a dumbass. After only a moment, Rainey bet on Eve's honesty with no more evidence for her belief than a gut feeling.

She called out, "Okay, I'm coming, but if someone takes a shot at me, you won't have to worry about anyone else coming down here to do you in. I'll do it myself."

"Please, please hurry," Eve begged.

Rainey whispered a reminder to herself, "Clear the corners and locate your targets."

She knelt and took a peek, exposing her head as far as she dared, but at a different level than a prospective shooter might anticipate. She gathered as much information as possible in the snapshot of time she was willing to remain visible.

The stairs led into an open space about twenty feet wide. The faux rock grotto wall continued on the left side to a corner where a bare hanging bulb glowed amber with age. About thirty feet away, against the far rock wall, a large white chest freezer stood next to a sparkling clean stainless steel prep station and sink, which sat under a wall-mounted display of shiny cleavers and knives on a long magnetic strip. Near the sink, an old, white-porcelain, six-burner stove gleamed from its apparent frequent polishing. Large heavyweight stockpots were stacked on restaurant style metal shelves beside it.

"It just get's better," Rainey whispered, her back against the stairway wall again.

"That looks like a cannibal's lair, for sure. A clean one, but still creepy as hell," she said to Eve.

"It's just where I prepare the food for myself and Sarabi."

"I assume Sarabi is the source of the roars I heard," Rainey said. "I have watched The Lion King at least once a month for the last two years.

One of my sons is obsessed with music and lions. It's the perfect combination for him. Simba's mother, Sarabi, right?"

While she talked, Rainey took another extended look. Following the rock wall around, she saw the bars of three cells on her right. Eugene sat slumped on a bale of hay where the far wall met the last set of bars and next to the stockpot shelves. If he didn't receive help soon, Rainey knew he would die, something she'd rather not happen. She wanted him alive to answer for his crimes and give multiple families closure.

On the wall above Eugene's head, an ankus hung beside the smashed skull of what Rainey suspected was Geordie, the lion OB killed with it. The skull included the broken lower jaw Chance said OB kept on his mantel. A lion pelt covered the floor at Eugene's feet. Those three things were physical evidence proving that house didn't go up accidently. OB would not have allowed the objects to be removed voluntarily. He was probably dead before the house exploded.

"Yes, Simba's mother, now hurry." Eve appealed to Rainey from the hidden area of the grotto. "You can't let him die. She'll kill my family. I swear she'll kill us all."

Rainey couldn't see Eve or much of the cell she occupied without stepping into full view of its occupant. Twenty-three years ago, on the day of her graduation from the FBI Academy, Billy Bell's advice to Rainey had been, "Okay, Rainey Blue, don't get dead." Those words echoed in her head before she gave a silent nod to her father's memory and turned the corner.

"Grraawwrr."

Rainey jumped back as a female lion leaped at the bars separating them.

"Sarabi, platz! Fuss, Sarabi. Hier!"

The lioness obeyed, "Sarabi down! Heel, Sarabi. Come!" which Rainey recognized as German training commands. They were common in security guard and K-9 training. Eve also asked Sarabi to "Zwinger bis," as Rainey understood it, "Kennel up." Eve opened a steel door between her cell and the next. The lioness moved into the middle cell, and the door closed behind her. Sarabi now had access to the other two cells but was closed off from the first. Once the lion had been secured, Eve approached the bars to stand in front of Rainey.

"That's impressive command of a wild animal without show of force," Rainey said to the woman on the other side of the bars.

Eve explained, "We have been together all her life. She trusts me. That is the only reason she does as I say."

Finally getting a look at Eve, Rainey saw a blonde, slim but not emaciated, and probably in her mid to late twenties. The cell she occupied appeared as if a tiny home had two walls replaced with bars—the one with the door and the one between it and the middle cell. The other two walls were of the same faux stone concrete design as the rest of the structure. The back wall of Eve's cell contained a small door like the one Rainey saw from the outside, allowing access to the outdoor area of the grotto. A twin bed sat on a frame with built-in storage drawers underneath. Walls not taken up by the small kitchenette and what appeared to be a curtained off bathroom area were covered in bookshelves. The entire place was spotless. This woman had been here a very long time.

Eve appealed to Rainey, "Please hurry. See the handle on the wall there. Pull the closest one to you. It's old, so pull hard."

"What does it do? You're not tricking me into opening the cell with the lion in it are you?"

"No, it opens my cell door. Hurry. I don't think Eugene is breathing anymore."

Rainey kept the Glock in her right hand, an eye on Eugene in case he was faking, and reached for the big metal handle with her left hand. There was no budging the handle that way. It was going to take both hands to make it move.

"Eve, may I see both of your hands on the bars, please. I have a spouse and kids. They would not want me to die because I trusted you and shouldn't have."

"You know you're really paranoid."

"Ass-hat over there was shooting at me and planted a bomb on a tiny house in which he locked my best friend's fiancé and my wife. Forgive me, if I'm as you say 'paranoid,' but Eugene is trying to kill me and the people I care about."

Eve looked confused. "You're married to a woman?"

"Yes," Rainey replied. Thinking it was not the time to discuss same sex marriage, she reiterated, "Hands please."

Eve's eyes widened. "Wow. I've missed a lot, I think," and then slipped her fingers around the bars in front of her with no further discussion.

Rainey took another glance at Eugene. She could see both of his hands, but not the weapon she knew he had. With no other choice, Rainey holstered her Glock, wrapped both hands around the handle, and pulled hard. Eve's cell door let out a long screeching creak as it opened one ear-piercing inch at a time. Rainey noted that Eugene didn't move, which meant he was either dead or unconscious.

"Holy cow," Rainey complained. "Don't you people have any oil around here?"

Eve answered with the matter-of-fact tone of someone resigned to fate. "It's just another level of security. How could I leave unannounced?"

She pointed at the top shelf in the corner of her cell. "Baby monitor. I can't breathe without someone hearing me."

Rainey had not seen the monitor. Aware now that they were under surveillance and her presence surely known by the monitoring entity, the need to get out of the grotto became more pressing.

Once the door to the cell opened, Eve gave Rainey little time to mull over the thought that she seemed familiar, as she pushed past her to go to Eugene. Rainey ran after Eve, arriving at her heels in time to see the revolver on the shelf over Eugene's head.

The lioness mirrored Rainey's movements on the other side of the bars, a low rumbling coming from its chest as it ran beside her. Rainey made eye contact with Sarabi, as she reached to secure Eugene's weapon. Representing the element of the brain to which fight or flight are the only choices, the lizard in her head reacted instinctively out of some ancient knowing, curled up in a ball, and played dead.

Rainey ignored the cowardly lizard's suggestion and remained standing, but made a cautious observation, "She's much bigger when you're this close."

Noise at the top of the stairs drew Sarabi's attention from Rainey. It also spun Rainey around and turned Eve's head.

"Well, well, well. Look what the cat drug in."

A unique and recognizably raspy voice accompanied the black leather boots Rainey could see descending the stairs.

"Don't shoot. You don't want me to push this little button and blow this grotto sky high. Your friends are still trying to disarm the IED on the tiny house. Oh, and I found the jammer remote in the garage when I rushed in to offer help after hearing the car crash into the building." She put on her fake personality, "Oh, dear God. What's happened? Hart? Oh, that can't be. Yes, I'll go call the police." The performance finished just as the woman came into view. Pleased with her reenactment and smiling at Rainey, she added, "I am so golden no matter what happens now."

Eve whispered low, "Naamah."

"Raarwwr. Hissssss." Sarabi reacted with unambiguous fear and loathing as the whip cracked in the air. "Raarwwrrr," the lioness warned, but backed away into the farthest corner of the cells as the woman appeared.

The sunglasses and scarf were gone, but Rainey recognized the voice of the person who stood at the bottom of the steps, a cell phone in one hand and a whip in the other.

"Ann? You're Naamah?" Rainey said astounded. "You're too young to be Eugene's mother."

"Correct, I am not his mother. I am Chance's mother. I am Eugene's sister. That cleft palate, an endearing trait of the inbred, made it hard to say 'Naomi' when he was young. I became Naamah to him forever, even after surgery corrected most of his pronunciation issues. Still has the damn lisp though, or had. Is he dead?"

"No, not yet," Rainey said, and then commented, "Naamah was a descendent of Cain who killed his brother, so I'm assuming the renaming was prophetic. You're not quite the Naomi from the good book either, that's for sure."

"Katie said you were smart and amusingly irreverent. I think that's the term she used."

"Naamah, huh. I thought Eugene was calling for his Momma. Is it okay if I just call you Ann?"

"Sure, you can call me whatever you like. As for Jean, we did away with her years ago. But before I explain, I need you to slide that revolver over here."

Rainey knelt to place Eugene's pistol on the floor, praying Ann would think it was the only one and not ask for the Glock.

"I'm going to need that weapon in your shoulder holster too. I understand you never leave home without it. Katie is a lovely woman, by the way."

"She is, and too trusting as well," Rainey said, while reluctantly placing her weapon next to Eugene's and then sliding them one by one to a spot a few feet in front of Ann.

Ann's hands were full. She kicked the two pistols into the middle cell, as she said, "This is true, but aren't most victims?"

"I haven't heard an explosion, so she's not your victim yet. I have faith in Captain Augustine that she can disarm the device," Rainey said. She would talk to this woman for as long as it took to figure out how to get out of this mess.

"Eve, slide Eugene's phone to me," Ann demanded.

Eve did as she was told, digging Eugene's phone out of the chest pocket of his flannel shirt. Rainey saw that the bullet went through the phone, shattering the screen and silencing the phone forever.

Eve slid the phone over to Ann, who reacted with, "Dammit! Eugene, you can never do anything right."

"Oh, that was me. Sorry about that. Bad aim. I was trying for center mass. But to my credit, Eugene was running," Rainey said, and then prodded Ann, "You were saying about his mother."

"Oh, you're cute. A smartass, but funny. I can see why Katie likes you so much. Now, about that body in the freezer in North Dakota, the one the police are having trouble sorting out, that's her. Did you know she was my mother and that she gave me to Obadiah when I was a child to do with as he pleased, just like her mother before her?"

"Jean was your mother too?"

150

"She was also Obadiah's child. He brought her mother, my grandmother, Gerda Löwenherz Burke, back from Germany after the war. She was found floating in the Eno when Jean was thirteen, a tragic accident they say. Jean had me when she was fourteen. Figure it out, profiler. What do you think happened?"

"Oh, wow. This family is more inbred than anything going on in 'Deliverance.' So, how did she get the name Berry? Who did she marry and what happened to him?"

"His name was Randy Berry. He owned the piece of land the garages sit on now. Obadiah wanted it. Randy inherited the property from his parents, Eugene and Cora Berry. My mother seduced Randy when she was already pregnant with little Eugene there, convinced him it was his child, and married him. He drowned in the Eno River at Sennett's Hole, supposedly diving for treasure in a sunken mill."

"Do you believe that story?"

"Old Jean took her secrets to the grave with her. She went to clean out the house in Pembina after I blew up Obadiah and the rest of the clan. She took Eugene and me with her. She didn't have a clue that I had caused the house explosion and that I blew up the garage with Joshua in it. Sorry about the agent. That wasn't supposed to happen."

"Supposed to or not, I don't think it mattered to his family," Rainey said.

Eve interrupted. "Since he's your brother or whatever, do you mind if I help Eugene? He appears to be dying."

Rainey caught the attitude in Eve's tone. She cared for Eugene, but Naomi/Naamah/Ann was reviled.

"Watch how you speak to me, Eve. Eugene can't protect you now."

The whip snapped, the lion growled and hissed, but Eve stood her ground.

"I'll not cower to you anymore. So lash me if you choose. I'm going to help him."

Rainey tried a distraction to prevent further harm to Eve or herself.

"I'm a profiler, as you say, Ann. Bombers aren't usually serial murderers. How does all this fit together?"

The diversion worked as Rainey surmised it would with a malignant narcissist like Ann. While she was occupied with Rainey's questions, Eve went about putting a pressure bandage on Eugene's shoulder. Again, Rainey felt a familiarity with Eve, but her main concern was buying them both more time. She listened as Ann volunteered information.

"Obadiah committed me to a mental institution. He would have killed me, but the neighbor had already called the police by the time he found me. That sort of put a wrench in his style of cleaning up family messes. I was pretty sure I was about to be another drowning victim."

Rainey remembered Chance's story about his mother trying to drown the boys. She commented on Ann's version of events.

"Like father, like daughter, eh? Weren't you about to drown your own child and two of Obadiah's other sons? Isn't that why you were hospitalized for ten years?

There appeared to be no remorse in Ann's answer of, "Yes. I decided no more of his sons would breed. I think I had a valid point. My therapist in the hospital agreed with my premise, but pointed out my method of birth control was a bit dramatic."

"I'd have to agree too, knowing what those men became," Rainey said before concluding, "They don't appear to have cured your homicidal tendencies before letting you go. How'd you manage a release?"

"I figured out how to convince people I was no longer a danger to others or myself. It took ten years, but I put the time to good use. I learned how to make IEDs from a crazy white supremacist and a fucked up Army guy. You'd be surprised what the mentally ill have to share if you just ask. I learned how to strip a skeleton, leaving nothing but those shiny white bones Eugene sent to you at the FBI."

"Why did you do that? Those missing person cases would have never been solved if you hadn't sent those bones to me. And why set up Chance. It had to be you, but why?"

"It's a family thing, you wouldn't understand."

"Oh, please, enlighten me. I've tried for nearly twenty years to figure this whole mess out. At least let me die with the truth, or your version of it anyway. "

Rainey couldn't believe she could have been so wrong about Chance. She wanted to know if her theories were that off. She was also banking on what she called the James Bond effect. The bad guy never just killed Bond. He had to tell him all about his crimes first. Rainey appealed to Ann's ego's need to explain how she had outsmarted the police and Rainey in particular.

Ann looked down at her cell phone. "Okay, I got a few minutes before all hell breaks loose up there, unless the Captain cuts the wrong wire." The smile she gave Rainey exposed her teeth and malice. "It's going to be a big one, but we're safe down here."

Rainey smiled back. "You weren't counting on Cathleen, were you?"

"No, but McNally would have scoured the earth for your killer. So it's working out well."

Rainey eyed the ankus on the wall. She glanced at the knives and wondered if her lack of cleaver throwing skills would impair her ability to immobilize Ann.

"Don't do it, Rainey. All I have to do is hit this green button on my phone and this grotto becomes a pile of blood stained rubble. You've profiled bombers. You know I'm not bluffing."

Rainey glared at her would be killer. "If that garage goes up while we're standing here, I'll make damn sure you and I go to hell together."

"Ooo, feisty. Katie said you were a badass."

"When I see her again, I'm going to talk to her about the concept of sharing too much with acquaintances."

"Awe, she loves you. It's sweet that she likes to brag on you a bit." Ann took a quick look at her phone and said, "Well, if you want to ask me questions about Chance, now's your chance." Ann chuckled at her word choices. "See what I did there?"

"You are not so clever," Rainey countered.

"Tick tock. You're wasting time being rude to me. I'll answer your questions as time permits. Go."

"Did Chance murder those women, the ones whose bones you sent to me?"

"No, but he did horrible things to them and then he gave them to me. I used old OB's bullhook to put them down and then Eugene threw them into the freezer for transport. Once they were frozen, he cut them up in the shop, and then fed the meat to his girls."

Ann's statement shocked Rainey with the implication that in addition to being lion food, the murder victims were also fed to Eve. Eve had claimed to prepare the meals there in the little kitchen where Rainey stood. That took a psychological disconnect which Rainey imagined was brought on by years of torture. She fought off the shudder, but not the facial expression that gave her revulsion away.

"That's right," Ann said. "Conquering armies have fed their victims to their forces for millennia. Crossing that line makes them more compliant with orders that would otherwise be unthinkable."

"Jesus, you are truly insane."

"Maybe, but like I said, I used my ten years locked up with the criminally insane to learn some things."

"Why would you clean up after Chance's crimes and then implicate him?"

"It wasn't motherly love. I kept his secrets. He kept mine. He knew about what I did to Jean and the others. But then he turned. That first box of bones was a way to remind him of his vulnerabilities." Ann chuckled and then said, "Damned if he didn't think it was a great idea. No DNA, you running around swearing it was him with no evidence, and I can guarantee, other than the bones sent to you, there is not one shred of those women left to find."

"Why did Eugene go along with killing his mother, your mother? It's so hard to keep up with relationships in your family."

"Robby and Chance gave Eugene some drug the night they got after that Dawson girl. Then, as he tells it, they forced him to do things to her. Chance said Eugene went at that girl like an animal with no prodding from his half-brothers."

"What does that have to do with Jean Berry?"

Ann's eyes narrowed, the hate obvious in her tone when she said, "Jean was OB's equal in brutality. She found out about the attack when the police questioned Eugene. Jean couldn't touch Robby or Chance. They were OB's to discipline. But Eugene was all hers to do with as she pleased. She read to him from the bible for six straight hours and then she cut his balls off."

Rainey shook her head. "Not one of you had a shot at being normal, did you?"

"No, not really. So to answer your question, Eugene hated Jean as much as I did. He hates those testosterone shots he has to take, too. My brother is a nice guy at heart. He was just born into hell."

"I don't know how nice he is. He tried to kill me twenty minutes ago."

"He will do anything to keep Eve, and I do mean anything. Chance nailed it when he said that girl there is Eugene's weakness."

"Bringing me back into this picture and the email today, the one that brought me here; was that Chance's idea, too?"

"Yep. Chance thought the Vanessa Wilhelm investigation would eventually lead to us, all of us. So, we set up Eugene to take the fall. It's working. I have to say, that boy of mine is a born evil genius."

"He's definitely evil. I'll give you that."

Rainey was troubled by the first murders. The bullhook was still in OB's possession at that point in the timeline, yet the wounds matched the I-95 corridor victims, the ones Ann claimed to have killed with OB's ankus.

"You were in the hospital when those bodies were put in the pond behind the house in Pembina. Who killed them?"

"That would have been the boys, Robby, Eugene, and Chance. Well, Robby and Chance raped and killed them. Eugene helped them dispose of the bodies."

"But the murder weapon was the same. Isn't that OB's bullhook hanging there? Isn't that what you said you used to kill the others? How did they have that if OB was still alive at the time?"

"Eugene. He's quite handy. He made a bullhook just like his father's. He wanted that mean old man to love him so badly. He tried hard to make it so."

"Did Eugene kill anyone?"

"No, he doesn't have the stomach for it. Eugene disposed of the bodies. They nearly got busted with that Emily Dawson girl. I explained the necessity to eliminate witnesses to Eugene, when he came crying to me about what Robby and Chance made him do."

"Wait, you were in the hospital when that happened."

"Eugene came with Jean to see me a few times when he was a kid. Later he came alone. He brought Robby and Chance to see me right before I got out."

"So, Vanessa Wilhelm did not inform Chance of your hospitalization."

"No, but she found out, and I'm quite sure in the end that she knew who I was. I have been passing as Jean Berry for nineteen years. It wasn't hard."

Rainey said, "You do look exactly like a younger version of your mother. The scarf and sunglasses worked. You were smart to wear them. I would have known who you were, or at least suspected something was wrong."

"It's those Prussian genes. They take age better than some."

"She wore such distinct makeup," Rainey said, all the while looking for a way out of the trap she'd fallen into.

"It was her signature look. I learned it early and found it was easy to fool the few people Jean had to meet in person to keep anyone from looking for her. I just became her. But that Wilhelm chick started coming around, asking to see Jean. She met me as Ann before I knew who she was. That complicated things."

Eugene groaned.

Eve said to Rainey, "Help me get him on the floor."

Rainey helped move Eugene, but she still had questions. "The rope and the knots were consistent through all the known murders. There were even little replicas tied around the bones that ended up at Quantico. Whose fetish was that?"

Eve surprised Rainey by answering, "It's how Eugene carried the bodies. He tied them up with the trucker's hitch, so they fit in the freezer unit on the truck and in here."

"This one," Ann said, pointing at Eve with the hand that held the whip. "Eugene had to have her. It was love at first sight for him."

"I can tell by Eve's living quarters that she's been here a while, or is she just one in a series of guests?"

Eve tended to her captor with such tenderness. Rainey struggled to understand, although she had known victims who believed they loved their abductors after years of captivity. This young woman had been a prisoner for a very long time to be able to forgive and forget how she came to be there.

"She was somewhere she shouldn't have been. Robby was there, Chance too. They didn't want her, but old Eugene here, he begged Chance not to snap her neck when she got too curious." She mocked her brother, "'Pleath, let me have thith one.' We gave in because it made Eugene part of the game, a game he could never stop playing the moment he took his little Eve home to this place where they will both perish."

"How long?" Rainey asked, beginning to see the end game.

Ann ignored her question. She began to slowly snake the whip around on the floor in front of her.

"Hiiissss. Rawrr."

"Shut up, you ungrateful beast," she said, as she snapped the whip at the cornered animal.

Sarabi rose on her hind legs and swung her great paws in the air.

"Raarrrrr. Grrrrrrr."

"Stop it," Eve shouted while cradling Eugene's head in her lap. "You cruel, evil, old witch."

Ann pulled the whip out of Sarabi's cell and raised it to strike at Eve. Rainey stepped between the two women, protecting Eve and Eugene from an assault.

"Oh, so you want to take her beating," Ann said, sneering at Rainey.

"No, I'd rather have my answer. How long has Eve been down here?"

"Ask her, she knows. She's kept a tally."

Eve looked up at Rainey and recited, "Nineteen years, two months, and twenty-five days."

Ann added, "That's right, Agent Bell. The source of the albatross around your neck, according to your lovely wife who loves to talk about her crime-fighting lover, has been alive all this time."

Rainey stared down at Eve, disbelieving what she was thinking. "Is your name Alyson Grayson?"

The woman Rainey knew as Eve blinked a wide-eyed expression at the hearing of her birth name. She turned to look at Ann, stricken with fear. It became evident to Rainey that Ann had tortured this woman if she used her real name. Just hearing it brought terror.

Rainey said to the woman with her kidnapper's head in her lap, "Your parents never stopped looking for you, Alyson. No matter what these people told you, your parents never gave up hope of finding you. They are waiting for you right now."

"Too bad," Ann said. "They'll read about how you tragically were found and killed in an explosion all in the same evening."

Alyson's expression of fear changed as she looked up at Rainey and asked the strangest question, "What does a cell jammer look like?"

Rainey said, "I don't know. Depends on the manufacturer, I guess."

Alyson held out her hand palm up with a small device resting on it. Rainey glanced at Ann, who looked stunned.

Alyson said, "She lies."

Rainey pulled the jammer detector from her pocket and saw the word, "Detected," on the screen.

Ann brought the whip up and began retreating toward the stairs. Alyson moved Eugene's head from her lap. She stood and took a step in front of Rainey, as if to protect her.

Rainey whispered behind Alyson, "Don't go after her. The police will catch her soon enough."

Ann laughed the obligatory laugh of maniacs about to kill. "The police will believe I knew nothing, that I am stunned by Hart's real identity, and will comfort me on those big, steroid extended shoulders they are so fond of building."

Ann stopped at the cell door controls. She had to tuck the whip under her arm in order to pull the door mechanism open for the unit where Sarabi panted in the corner. Rainey began a move to prevent Ann from opening the door; worried about the lioness forgetting which one of them she hated the most.

Alyson grabbed Rainey's arm, stopping her, and said. "Stay behind me."

The screeching metal on metal sent a shudder through Rainey. It was a foreboding announcement that death was coming at the hands of a madwoman or a mad lion. Neither appealed to Rainey, as she made a move for the cleavers, but froze on Alyson's command to the still cowered lioness.

"Hier! Sarabi."

The big cat obeyed, bounding so close her tail slapped against Rainey's leg.

"Oh my God. Oh my God," Rainey whispered to no one.

Alyson reached behind her to pull Rainey close, while saying, "Calm yourself."

Ann did not appear to have anticipated Alyson's complete control of the animal. She quickly pulled the whip and snapped a loud crack in the air.

"Raawwrr," Sarabi responded.

Alyson shouted, "Sarabi, töte sie. Fass! Fass!"

Ann tried to swing the whip again, but it made no difference. Sarabi sprang and covered the distance between them in one flying leap. Ann tried to turn and run. Sarabi knocked her prey to the floor, grabbed her by the neck, and sunk her teeth in deep.

Alyson said, "Stay here," to Rainey and then casually walked to the cell door controls. She pulled the center lever. The door slid open. Alyson entered the cell, retrieved the weapons Ann had kicked there, and then returned to the controls.

"Gute, Sarabi. Gute," Alyson said to the purring cat.

Ann wasn't moving. Rainey surmised Sarabi's teeth had found their mark at the base of her skull. Alyson pushed the lever in that closed the cell door near Rainey and the still breathing, but barely, Eugene.

She then directed Sarabi, "Zwinger bis."

The lioness dragged her prey into the center cell. Alyson closed the door behind her. Rainey let out the breath she had been holding.

"Let's get out of here. I'm sure she wasn't lying about this place being rigged to blow up."

Rainey began moving toward the staircase, stopping to collect the weapons from Alyson, who stood by the cell door levers taking a long last look at her prison. She focused on Eugene for a second and then reopened the cell door next to where he lay. She then turned to follow Rainey out of the grotto without a single comment.

As Rainey pushed the big steel door at the top of the stairs shut and latched it, Alyson said, "She won't eat them, unless no one comes to feed her. They will come, won't they?"

"I'll make sure she's taken care of, Alyson. She deserves that."

Alyson made a request, as they walked toward the exit, "Don't let them kill her. I read there are sanctuaries. Is that real? Can Sarabi go live in a sanctuary?"

"I think we can arrange that," Rainey answered.

"And can I really talk to my mom?"

"Yes, Alyson. I know she's been waiting for this phone call for a long time."

As they exited through the chain-link fence gate, Alyson looked around at the trees and then down at the ground. "I haven't felt real earth under my feet in so long, I forgot what it felt like."

"Rainey!" Danny's voice cut through the forest.

"Over here!" she replied.

"Rainey!" Katie called, just before a bank of flashlights came into view, heading toward Rainey's position.

"We're here," she yelled. She dug out her flashlight from her jacket pocket and waved it in the air. She turned to Alyson. "You see those lights, Alyson Grayson. That's your rescue party. That's your ticket home."

Alyson smiled up at Rainey and said, "I think we did all right rescuing ourselves."

"Right you are, Alyson. Well done." Rainey put her arm around the shorter woman's shoulders. "By the way, how did you learn how to train a lion, in German no less?"

"Naamah thought it would be more torture to give me only old books written in German for the first few years I was here. I lived in a truck trailer for the first year. I was only allowed out at night. Eugene gave me a German-English dictionary. Later he gave me videos of German movies. I had nothing to do but teach myself to read and speak the language."

"And Sarabi? Was she with you the whole time?"

"I had just been moved into my cell when Naamah brought Sarabi to the grotto. I raised her. I fed her. I am her mother. I did everything for her, just like in the book on lion training said. Sarabi would only answer to me because neither of them spoke the only language I ever used with her."

"You are a brilliant young woman, Alyson Grayson. Your mother was right about you. She said you'd never give up."

"Gib nicht auf! Es gibt immer Hoffnung."

Rainey laughed. "I'm going to need a translator."

"Do not give up," Alyson said. "There is always hope."

Rainey hugged Alyson to her side, as the flashlights grew nearer, and said, "Always, my new friend. Always."

19

Rainey sat on a bench in the Emergency Room hallway, waiting for Danny to come back. She stared at her phone, reading the scores and watching video from the basketball games she missed.

"The kids are great at Mom and Dad's for another night. Mom is going to take them to The Museum of Life and Science," Katie said, as she sat next to Rainey. "We have the day and evening to recover from our ordeal."

Rainey put the phone in her pocket and reached for Katie's hand. "That's good. Although, I'm sorry I'm missing out. I love going there with them."

"You'll get plenty of chances before they lose interest in going anywhere with you," Katie said, and then yawned.

"You need a nap."

Katie put her head on Rainey's shoulder. "Just wake me up when it's time to go home. How much longer?"

"There is someone from psych in there with her now. I think they should keep her for a few days, but that's not up to me."

"She seemed healthy, but I know the damage is more than physical," Katie said. "I can't believe she kept asking if Hart, or Eugene, or whoever he really is, was alive."

Rainey looked over her shoulder at the door to the private trauma room used for SART exams. Alyson had been submitted to a barrage of questions from law enforcement, Emergency Room personnel, and now a psychiatrist.

Rainey put her arm around Katie and pulled her closer, before explaining, "He was her only human contact that did not come with violence for the last nineteen years, two months, and twenty-five days. Eugene brought food and companionship. He comforted her when Ann brought nothing but pain and terror. Alyson depended on Eugene for everything from water to access to her basic human hygiene needs. He was her world, well, him and Sarabi."

Katie yawned through the first part of her comment. "I'm so glad that veterinarian from State College was able to dart her. Thank you for not letting them shoot her. Where are they taking her?"

"The vet said she got in touch with the zoo and they have a quarantine area Sarabi can stay in while she is evaluated. They have to decide what the best placement options are."

"There you are," Sergeant Detective Sheila Robertson approached wearing a big smile. "Danny told me you were here at the hospital."

Rainey started to stand, but Sheila waved her off.

"Sit, sit." She leaned down to give Katie and Rainey both hugs. "I am so glad you were not blown up or eaten by a lion."

Rainey smiled up at her old friend. "You and me both."

"I came by to give you the news personally. We did get a hit on the Gaskill DNA, but it isn't Chance Hale."

Rainey said it before Sheila could. "It was his half-brother, Robby Hughes."

"Damn. You take the fun out of everything. How did you know?"

"A crazy woman told me," Rainey said.

"Did she tell you that we got more hits and I've just solved a serial rapist case that spans—"

"—nearly twenty years." Rainey finished the sentence for Sheila with a grin, and then offered, "Congratulations. Are they going to prosecute?"

"We have a few willing victims whose assaults are still within the statute of limitations. If he recovers, he'll do it inside a state institution and not that posh care facility he's currently in."

"I know those women will be pleased to know he's drooling on himself, but they would probably rather he do that behind bars."

Katie joined the conversation with, "I know I would."

Sheila shook her head from side to side. "It just kills me that we could have had him sooner. I had a warrant for his DNA ready to be signed back in '98, but Tammy's parents pushed her to back off her story. I think they were paid off. We got Robby on the drug charge, but the judge wouldn't sign the DNA warrant without victim cooperation. I suspect he was paid off too. OB Hale was a son of a bitch."

Rainey chuckled, "I've heard that more than once this weekend."

The automatic doors of the ER entrance opened with a "woosh."

A woman, slight of build and rather short, walked in followed by Danny and another man. Rainey recognized the woman immediately. Marilyn Grayson had aged, but her resemblance to her daughter was unmistakable. She made eye contact with Rainey, which turned into a moment of realization for her.

Katie must have felt the tension in Rainey's muscles because she moved out of the way without being asked so that Rainey could stand.

Marilyn Grayson sped her steps and came to stand in front of Rainey.

"I've wanted to tell you something for a long time, former Agent Bell, as I was informed you had left the Bureau when I called to check on Alyson's case four years ago. I lived on your promise the promise that you would find her for years. Then I hated you for giving me hope." Tears ran down Marilyn's cheeks, as she paused to gather herself, before continuing, "But you found her, and I'm so sorry I ever doubted you, that I cursed you and despised you for so long."

"Don't apologize, Mrs. Grayson. If it helped you get through the bad days, I'm glad you had somewhere to put your anger."

Rainey fought back empathetic tears, but she could see Katie was making no effort to stop hers. As the man with Danny approached, Rainey saw that it was Alyson's father, Allen. He didn't have anything to say. He walked up to Rainey and hugged her so tight she thought her ribs would bust.

When Allen released her from his grip, Marilyn asked, "Is she okay? Can we see her?"

"A representative of the psychiatric unit is with her now. She should be out soon. I know Alyson is anxious to see you both."

"I can't believe she survived all this time." Marilyn dug in her purse for a tissue and wiped her tears away while asking Rainey, "What did he do to her? Do you know?"

Rainey answered with cautions for Alyson's parents. "I'm sure Agent McNally explained everything we know. There is so much we don't know. It will be up to Alyson to speak about her captivity on her own terms, if ever. I'd advise you to listen if she wants to talk and let go of your need to know if she doesn't share with you."

Allen asked, "Can we take her home?"

"I'm not the one to ask, Mr. Grayson, but speaking from experience, Alyson needs some time to process. Going home right away might be too much stimulus at once. A few days here in the hospital would do wonders for her recovery and give you both time to get to know your daughter before you go home and face friends and family, not to mention the press and all the people who will come out of the woodwork to get a piece of this story."

The obvious disappointment clouded both parents' faces.

"I also need to caution you about your first meeting. In your mind, Alyson is still fourteen. She never grew up for you. She is a thirty-three-year-old woman now. Be prepared for that." Rainey paused to smile at Marilyn. "She looks a lot like I remember you looking nearly twenty years ago."

Allen had other things on his mind. "And the man that did this? Is he dead?"

"No, sir. He's in surgery. Your daughter saved his life."

Allen Grayson looked like he'd been slapped. "She saved him, after what he did to her?"

Rainey held her hands up in the surrender pose. "I understand how confusing this can all be. Alyson isn't the only one that needs to process. You both will benefit from therapy sessions with her and individually. Please, trust me, like you did when I said we would find her. Therapy may sound trivial, but it will be the only way your family survives."

Marilyn nodded in agreement. "We'll be in therapy, all of us."

Allen wasn't in that headspace yet. He was still looking to punish someone. "Agent McNally said this was a family of serial murderers. Are they all accounted for now? There aren't any more of them out running the streets where they can tear other families apart, are there?"

Danny answered, "Robby Hughes is a drooling mess from a drug overdose, but even so, he is headed to some sort of state facility for the criminally insane, according to Sergeant Detective Sheila Robertson." He pointed at Sheila who acknowledged the Graysons with a nod. "Eugene will face prosecution on multiple charges and will never be free again. As for Chance Hale, they'll be taking him back to Florida Monday morning to stand trial on murder and rape charges down there. He may not have personally killed those women, but he is complicit in a felony that resulted in their deaths. Then he'll have a date with Maine, South Carolina, Delaware, Massachusetts, and Virginia."

Rainey added, "That accounts for the known members of the Hale clan."

"Known members? There could be more?" It was Katie who wanted this information.

Danny helped Rainey out by trying to assuage Katie's concerns. "As far as we know, there are no more living Hale family members."

Katie was not that easy to persuade, as Rainey knew. She almost chuckled at Danny's expression when Katie came back at him with, "That's not very reassuring, Danny."

Marilyn said, "I'm with her."

The door to the trauma room opened, and the doctor stepped out holding her clipboard in one hand and a cell phone to her ear with the other.

"Yes, a private room. Don't argue with me. This is medically necessary." She listened for a few seconds, and then said, "Thank you. We'll be going up in about ten minutes."

She put her phone away and turned to the group. "Hello, I'm Dr. Neumann. Are any of you Alyson's parents?"

Allen and Marilyn stepped forward, saying simultaneously, "We are."

"I need to speak with you before you go in. We can talk in private across the hall here."

Alyson's parents started following Dr. Neumann before Marilyn suddenly turned and hurried back to hug Rainey.

"I will never be able to repay you for not giving up on Alyson. God bless you, Rainey Bell. Thank you for bringing her back to us. Thank you for rescuing her for us."

Rainey knew she hadn't been the catalyst in this rescue. It was Chance's need to get rid of Eugene and his mother that involved her again. She was just a pawn in the battle of the Hales for supremacy. Marilyn didn't need to know all that today.

Rainey smiled and replied, "Like Alyson said, she did a pretty good job of rescuing herself last night. That is an amazing young woman in there. You'll be proud of the survivor she has become."

Marilyn made her way across the hall to join the doctor and her husband behind a closed door.

Sheila spoke first, "Well, I'm glad you didn't get dead, Rainey Bell. You too, Katie. McNally, the Bureau is going to miss you, but I'm happy you'll be a permanent fixture around here."

"Me too," Danny said. "Although, I am concerned about hanging with these two magnets of mayhem."

Katie pointed at Rainey, saying, "It's her."

Rainey laughed. "Who hired the murderers to build tiny houses for the center? Are my background checks too burdensome now, little missy?"

Katie countered with, "But I was just collateral damage. They were after you."

The group started moving toward the door to the parking lot.

Rainey answered Katie, "And if you didn't think I was so paranoid, you would have let me run checks on them before you started telling my would-be murderers where I keep my weapon. What all did you tell Ann about me?"

Rainey heard Sheila say, "Are you sure about being neighbors?"

Danny laughed. "I wouldn't want to be anywhere else."

Cathleen waited outside. She stood when she heard them coming.

Rainey stopped debating with Katie long enough to do what she had promised back at the grotto. With all the questions from investigators, dealing with Sarabi, and getting Alyson to the hospital, she had not had time to thank Cathleen properly. She ran over to her, lifted her off the ground, spun her around, and planted a kiss on her lips.

"I promised myself if you saved my girl here, I was going to give you a kiss. Thank you, Captain Augustine. I am forever in your debt."

Sheila elbowed Danny. "I'll ask again, are you sure you want her living that close to you. You know what they say about women, they're only straight until they're not."

Cathleen winked at Rainey and said, "Don't ask. Don't tell, right."

Katie kept walking and called over her shoulder. "Don't worry, Danny. We won't keep her. We just need a new toaster."

About the Author

Four-time Lambda Literary Award Finalist in Mystery—*Rainey Nights* (2012), *Molly: House on Fire* (2013), *The Rainey Season* (2014), and *Relatively Rainey* (2016)—and 2013 Rainbow Awards First Runner-up for Best Lesbian Novel, *Out on the Panhandle,* author R. E. Bradshaw began publishing in August of 2010. Before beginning a full-time writing career, she worked in professional theatre and also taught at both university and high school levels. A native of North Carolina, the setting for the majority of her novels, Bradshaw now makes her home in Oklahoma. Writing in many genres, from the fun southern romantic romps of the Adventures of Decky and Charlie series to the intensely bone-chilling Rainey Bell Thrillers, R. E. Bradshaw's books offer something for everyone.

CPSIA information can be obtained
at www.ICGtesting.com
Printed in the USA
FSOW02n0338250817
37981FS